WHAT GOES UP

WHAT GOES UP

WEN JANE BARAGREY

Random House New York

Text copyright © 2018 by Wen Jane Baragrey
Jacket art copyright © 2018 by Stevie Lewis

All rights reserved. Published in the United States by Random House Children's Books, a division of Penguin Random House LLC, New York.

Random House and the colophon are registered trademarks of Penguin Random House LLC.

Visit us on the Web! rhcbooks.com

Educators and librarians, for a variety of teaching tools, visit us at RHTeachersLibrarians.com

Library of Congress Cataloging-in-Publication Data
Name: Baragrey, Wen Jane, author.
Title: What goes up / Wen Jane Baragrey.
Description: Robyn Tinkerbell Goodfellow, twelve, lives in a house that seems to attract trouble, so when a satellite is expected to crash she races to learn the truth about her long-lost father before it is too late.
Identifiers: LCCN 2017034839 | ISBN 978-1-5247-6581-1 (hardcover) | ISBN 978-1-5247-6584-2 (hardcover library binding) | ISBN 978-1-5247-6583-5 (ebook)
Subjects: Identity—Fiction. | Single-parent families—Fiction. | Family Life—Fiction. | Artificial satellites—Fiction.
Classification: LCC PZ7.1.B3678 Wh 2018 | DDC [Fic]—dc23

The text of this book is set in 12.25-point Sabon MT Pro.
Interior design by Jaclyn Whalen

Printed in the United States of America
10 9 8 7 6 5 4 3 2 1
First Edition

For Jayden, the smallest person I ever looked up to

CHAPTER 1

When my bare foot touched the rickety boards of our front step, a man's voice came from somewhere high above me.

"Hello down there!"

I squealed and held up my hands in a classic self-defense position. "Identify yourself!"

Things landed on our house all the time: balls, kites, and even our neighbor's giant tree. None of those things had ever talked to me.

"I'm real sorry to bother you, little girl, but I could use some help."

"I'm not a little girl. I'm practically twelve," I said, my heart thumping hard. "If you're trying to break into our house, you should know I invented the art of Focus Pocus, and I have a black belt." The truth was, my best friend had invented it, but I'd been there and helped by surviving the first-ever Focus Pocus Doom Glare. It wouldn't do much to stop a determined burglar, but it might confuse him a little.

"I have no idea what Focus Pocus is, and I'm not trying to steal anything. I'm a bit lost. If you would call nine-one-one, I'd be very grateful," he said.

Since a thief wouldn't ask for 911, my heart settled a bit. I pushed my glasses back on my nose, shaded my eyes, and squinted upward. There, dangling by his harness from my grandma's rooster weather vane, was an embarrassed-looking skydiver.

"Could you throw down a Frisbee or two while you're up there?" I asked.

He looked at his swinging feet. "Not without falling."

I sighed.

There were probably toys on that roof from when Grandma was a kid. I could have made a fortune selling them on the school black market if I could've gotten them down. But Grandma was terrible with heights, and Mom couldn't be trusted with a ladder. The treasure was so close, but there was no way for me to get my hands on it.

Half an hour later, the fire department was trampling all over Grandma's roses. They used to grow in neat rows beside the path until she felt sorry for them and set them free. Now they straggled everywhere in random tangles.

Chief Watson marched over to greet me. On the way, his boot caught in one of the drooped-over rosebushes.

His arms flailed and his helmet slipped sideways, but he stayed upright and managed a smile. Thanks to my strict Focus Pocus training, I kept my cool and didn't giggle, but it was a close one.

"How goes life beneath the magnet roof, Robyn?" he asked, winking at me. We were practically friends, since he had been to our house more often than the mailman.

"It's okay, except for skydivers and nosy neighbors," I said.

Chief Watson's eyes twitched toward Mrs. Cuthbert's house. Since Mrs. Cuthbert thought she was a special undercover operative for the FBI, she would for sure be peering through her binoculars at us. If anyone even looked in her direction, she'd take that as an invitation to come and run things. In other towns, people probably called the police to report neighbors like meddlesome Mrs. Cuthbert. In Calliope, you left your neighbors alone, because chances were if they moved, you'd end up with someone way odder. I wasn't sure there could be anyone worse than Mrs. Cuthbert.

The chief patted the pom-pom of hair in the ponytail on top of my head. "Hang in there, kiddo."

Grandma arrived home in the middle of all the fuss, carrying a paper bag filled with groceries.

"Watch where you put those ladders, Davy Watson!" Grandma growled as she elbowed her way through the small crowd of busybodies gathered at our front gate. Chief Watson saluted her as she hurried by, but she didn't even stop to wave.

Grandma took my arm and herded me through the front door and into the room that used to be our living room but now was a fairy-themed party room. These days we watched TV in the kitchen, and Mom hosted parties in her homemade Fairy Wonderland. Papier-mâché forest critters peered out at us from behind giant toadstools and fake weeping willows with gauzy leaves.

They had taken Mom months to make. She still painted over the animals' eyes sometimes, trying to get them to look focused.

Today she sat cross-legged on the low party table she had painted to look like a rock with ivy vines. She was turning paper napkins into small folded fairies. "Ooh, the fire department is here," she said, placing her latest fairy in a basket with dozens of others.

"Did you hear the news, Mary?" Grandma whispered to Mom, like it was a big secret.

"News? Not if I can help it. Too depressing." Mom unfolded herself from the table and stretched out her back. "I should go and supervise the firefighters." She tapped my shoulder with her wand, leaving sparkles all over my T-shirt.

"Hush," Grandma said. "NASA said one of their satellites has gone rogue and will crash back to Earth sometime soon. A month at most, they reckon."

Mom shrugged. "So?"

A little shiver wriggled through me. Satellites were a lot bigger and heavier than skydivers or kites. Even a roof that was used to things landing on it might struggle with an out-of-control satellite.

Grandma and I looked through the window at the firefighters lowering the skydiver to the ground. Everyone ducked to avoid a Frisbee he knocked loose, as it looped the loop on its way down.

"Oh, the magnet roof. I see," Mom said. "Don't let that worry you. I doubt it can attract satellites."

Grandma sniffed. "Why shouldn't it land here? This is as good as any other house."

Sometimes when Mom and Grandma said "I love you," it came out sounding like an argument. Truth was, they only argued for the fun of it. They agreed on most everything, and I could tell that neither of them took this problem seriously.

"Maybe we should move," I said.

Mom waggled her very realistic-looking fairy wings at me. My mother wore fairy wings and a tutu every day, even to pick me up from school. Lucky for me, there were stranger moms in Calliope. Well, *as* strange, anyway.

"I've got ten kids coming in the morning," Mom said.

"We'd never find another house with space for parties. I can't move the Fairy Wonderland."

She had a point. The animals and trees would be pretty hard to fit in a moving van.

Mom half skipped, half danced outside to wave her wand at the firefighters as they packed up the fire truck.

"I was born in this house, and it'll take more than a satellite to get rid of me," Grandma said. "This old house can stand up to anything. Your mom and I have rebuilt all the damaged parts over the years. It's solid as they come."

That didn't help at all. While Grandma was great at building things, Mom was another story. We still used a spice rack she had put together. It had come with instructions even I could understand, but instead of keeping her jars of herbs and spices neat and tidy, it flung them out into the kitchen like tiny out-of-control satellites.

We were doomed.

CHAPTER 2

I followed Grandma into the kitchen. It was the biggest room in the house, so we used it as our living room as well. It worked fine in winter, when the stove kept the whole room warm, but in summer it felt like a sauna around mealtimes.

Grandma took down a pot and a bunch of herbs that hung over the sink.

"Mrs. Cuthbert's tree smashed a huge hole in the house," I said, gripping the edge of the kitchen counter.

"The house wouldn't stand for that sort of nonsense twice," Grandma said with a shrug, sliding the biggest chopping knife out of the knife block. "It was pure bad luck, that's all."

"What if we get bad luck again?"

Grandma chuckled and leaned her hip against the sink. "I bet the satellite would bounce."

"Bounce! How could it bounce? The roof is metal, and

a satellite is metal—I guess—and metal doesn't bounce. It would just burn a hole right through, wouldn't it?" I gasped for breath, pushing my glasses farther up on my nose. "This isn't a joke."

Grandma patted my nose with a bunch of chives. "You, Robyn Tinkerbell Goodfellow, are a born pessimist."

Reminding me of my embarrassing middle name did nothing to help, but Grandma was too busy humming to herself while she rinsed the herbs to answer any more questions. I dumped my backpack onto the part of the kitchen sofa where the springs stuck out, flopped into my favorite spot, and flicked on the television.

"Do I hear the TV?" Mom yelled from the porch. Dealing with sugar-rushed toddlers all day gave her lightning-fast reflexes and bionic hearing. She preferred I do something creative to stretch my brain in the afternoons, but my brain already felt as stretchy as pizza cheese.

"Nope," Grandma called back, winking at me.

I flipped through the channels until I found one that looked interesting. Thanks to Grandma's rejecting anything but public stations, the best we had was the local news.

"NASA predicts the XR-26 satellite's orbit will continue to deteriorate until the craft reenters Earth's atmosphere sometime in June. For now, scientists believe the satellite has a low chance of making landfall," said the news anchor. I could tell by her serious expression that she did not believe that story any more than I did.

My stomach tightened into a nervous little ball. When Mrs. Cuthbert chopped down her ancient sycamore tree the previous year, it had smashed my bedroom wall and ceiling to splintereens. I would have died if I'd been in bed. A satellite had farther to fall and would hit a lot harder than a tree.

Something went *ping-zip* near the stove. Grandma yelped, and a tiny thing whizzed through the air near my head. The ancient glass vase on the coffee table exploded into a million flying shards. I threw myself backward onto the sofa, grabbing at my chest and gasping for air.

"Stupid spice rack! My mother gave me that vase!" Grandma panted, hurrying over to sweep up the mess. She patted my knees, which were curled up near my nose. "Oh, Sparkles. Don't look so worried. You heard them. They say the satellite's going to land in the ocean. Even if they're wrong, I'm positive this house can withstand any satellite NASA throws at it. You'll see."

It couldn't stop a tree.

By the time Grandma swept up the last of the glass, the news had finished and *What's Current* had come on. I crossed my fingers for something a bit less nerve-racking than killer satellites, like "The Calliope Pedigree-Cat Show" or "Mr. Wilkins Grew a Giant Eggplant."

I did not get it.

A dark-haired woman with very red lips smiled at the camera, a microphone in her hands. "Last weekend, Calliope's Towne Park played host to a most unusual family get-together. Three generations of the O'Malley family gathered for a picnic, as they do at a new location every month."

The screen showed a shot of the park, followed by a view of several picnic tables sagging under a ton of food.

"Against very steep odds, many of the O'Malley grandchildren have been born with albinism, a rare inherited condition that often causes visual problems as well as very pale skin and blue eyes. It certainly produces a striking family resemblance."

Shaking, I pointed the remote at the TV and lowered the sound until I was sure Grandma couldn't possibly hear it over her banging pots and pans. Albinos. Like me. I'd asked Mom and Grandma a million times where I had gotten my albinism, since both of them had dark hair and decent tans. Mom said that both parents had to have the gene for a child to have it, and the parents' skin tone didn't matter. But no one else in Mom's family had albinism. Only me.

Maybe the gene was stronger in my dad's family. Or maybe the O'Malleys *were* his family! After all, how many families with albinism could live so close by? But Mom wouldn't tell me anything about him except that I reminded her of him. I'd never even met him. I thought I never would.

The next shot showed a class-field-trip-sized group of kids of different ages. Quite a few of them had the same hair as mine, pale as moonlight and curly as a bucketful of springs under their sun hats. The remote control toppled out of my fingers and onto the floor.

Surely there were more people like me out there than just this one family. But how many of them had frizzy spirals for hair? Because every one of the kids filmed in Towne Park that day did. I could have slipped in and shared the picnic without looking a bit out of place, and I always looked out of place. Always. Even though I was lucky with my albinism and only needed to take care in the sun and wear glasses, I still stood out.

The story ended and a new one came on, but I stared straight ahead until my eyeballs nearly dried out. If the reporters mentioned the satellite again, I didn't hear it. I barely heard Grandma ask if I wanted her extra-special, personally invented Plum Pullover for dessert.

During dinner, Mom peered at me over the top of a spoon loaded with plums. "What's wrong, kiddo? You haven't said a word all through dinner."

I couldn't tell her about the O'Malleys. Nothing made my mom clam up faster than when I mentioned my dad. "Nothing."

"It'll be the satellite thing," Grandma said.

I groaned. That too.

Mom waved her hand in the air as if it still had her wand in it. "I shall cast a shield of fairy dust over the house to protect us all." Sometimes I wondered if Mom was artistic, like she said, or downright peculiar, like Grandma said.

I rested my cheek on my hand and poked at my food. I had almost forgotten about the stupid satellite, thanks to the O'Malleys. My dad had to be one of them, which meant I had to be one of them too. All I had to do now was figure out how to find him before the satellite flattened me.

One month was a long time when it came right before Christmas or my birthday, but it was no time at all with a satellite hurtling toward my house.

• • •

After sunset and bedtime cookies, I trudged up the stairs in a terrible mood. Mom appeared from her workroom and followed me to my door, grinning a grin almost as wide as her whole face.

"Can I help you?" I asked.

"I thought I'd tuck you in."

Technically, Focus Pocus masters weren't supposed to be tucked in after they were ten years old, but we had made up that rule before we knew about satellites. "Shouldn't I get into my pj's first?"

She reached in front of me and grabbed the door handle. "In a minute."

The door swung open. I blinked, then blinked again.

Glowing stars covered every space on the walls and ceiling. Dozens of them, like small colorful galaxies. The most amazing thing, though, hung right in the middle of the ceiling.

A large white paper moon, glowing brighter than all the stars, real and pretend. Fluffy clouds floated around it and caught the moonlight.

"You did this?" I whispered.

Mom wrapped her arms around me. "You were worried about the satellite, so I thought I'd remind you how beautiful the universe is."

When the lights came on, I saw she had stuck toy glow-in-the-dark stars over my posters and new wallpaper. The moon was just a white paper lampshade with a solar garden light inside, and the cotton wool clouds hung on strands of thread from the ceiling. I didn't care. Once you believed in magic, it didn't matter if you saw the strings.

I got into my pj's at top speed and jumped into bed. Mom switched off the light, and my own personal universe glowed back to life and swayed in the darkness around me.

"It's like I'm the satellite," I said.

"No. You're the star." Mom gave me a smooch on the forehead and waved good night.

"Wait, Mom," I said, plucking up all my nerve. I had to try.

She turned back from the door and smiled. "Hmm?"

"Do you think my dad might be wondering if we're okay? You know, with the satellite coming and all?"

Her smile didn't move. At all. It froze there on her face and didn't match her eyes anymore. "They said it will land in the ocean. We'll be safe."

"But my dad might be worried, though?"

"Sweet dreams," she whispered, and backed out of the room.

I watched the moon wobble slowly among the fading stars while I waited for its power to run out. I tried to relax, but whenever I drifted off, one of the glowing stars turned into a satellite-shaped missile, sped across the room, and tore the paper moon to shreds.

CHAPTER 3

Mrs. Gilbert's English class was first thing in the morning. Because she also taught drama, her reading assignments were often plays. This time it was *A Midsummer Night's Dream*, which was about—oh, joy—fairies.

"It's my favorite of Shakespeare's plays," she said. Since everyone in Calliope knew everything about everyone else in Calliope, Mrs. Gilbert smiled right at me. "I think you'll love this one, Robyn."

Every face in the room turned to me, some sniggering.

Mrs. Gilbert passed the books around, and we opened them to the first page.

If Shakespeare had spoken English, it was a kind of English I had never heard before. I threw my hand up into the air and wriggled my fingers around. Mrs. Gilbert beamed, as if any question I had would be the best question ever.

"Yes, Robyn?"

"I think you accidentally gave me a foreign version," I said.

The smile on Mrs. Gilbert's face wobbled as she peered at me over her glasses. "It is English. Maybe it's different from the way we speak today, but it's still English."

The class giggled again, which was not fair, since I bet none of them understood it either.

I stared down at words like "methinks" and "betwixt" until my eyes ached. After two entire minutes of squinting, I skipped over the words I didn't understand. The reading went a lot faster but made no more sense.

Until something caught my eye.

A name.

Robin Goodfellow. One of the lead characters had both my names, and he—yes, *he*—was a fairy.

For years I had coped with having Tinkerbell for a middle name because I had thought the rest of my name was normal. But, no, Mom had fooled me and gotten away with it for almost twelve whole years.

Seconds later, everyone else must have made it to the same place in the book as I had, because the giggles and whispers started up again.

Dameon Swenson, who never missed a chance to poke fun, pointed at me and cried, "Puck! Hockey puck!" like it was the most hilarious thing in the world.

Everyone else laughed like it was. If the satellite

squished me, people would be too busy laughing at my name to care about the tragedy of it all.

My cheeks grew hotter by the second, but I knew I had gotten off lightly. Any mother willing to name her kid after a fairy could have done a lot worse. Tinkerbell could have been my first name.

My best friend, Nickel, turned around in his seat. "Your mother named you aft—"

My Focus Pocus Doom Glare froze his mouth shut.

Turning each page with a slap, I scowled at the words. Stupid play. Stupid fairies.

Looking apologetic, Nickel reached back and slipped me a note. I tucked it inside the book to wait until something distracted Mrs. Gilbert. Of all the teachers in the whole school, she was the one I did not want to catch me passing notes. She read them to the class before posting them in the school newspaper.

It was the most popular column. It had the juiciest gossip and the best comeback material all in the same place. The worst part was that the newspaper went home to the parents. If your note got confiscated, you had better hope you'd written about how hard you planned to study.

My chance to read Nickel's message came near the end of class, when Mrs. Gilbert stepped outside to talk to another teacher. I flipped open the scrap of paper inside the book to keep any busybodies like Dameon from seeing it and turning me in.

Nickel's handwriting made almost as much sense as Shakespeare's English. After some squinting at one word that could have been either "tonight" or "toothless," I decided the note said this:

Leaving school after this class—doctor's visit.
Wanna come to the movies in Densdale tonight?
Mom's driving. I'm paying.

Nickel always paid. He had a little sister called Penny and an older brother called Dime. The names must have worked, because they were the richest family in Calliope, which Mom always said was like a magic trick on a cop's salary.

Money was not my problem, though. Densdale was.

In Calliope, we were supposed to pretend Densdale didn't exist. Calliope started out as a separate town, but the city of Densdale grew all around until Calliope became just another suburb. Except the locals refused to believe that and kept right on as if the city was something that happened to other, less stubborn people. True Calliopeans bought what they needed in Calliope or drove over an hour to the next city to get it, rather than shop in Densdale.

The story goes that Mrs. Cuthbert's other neighbor, Mrs. Humphries, had her baby in the back of her husband's van rather than stop at Densdale General Hospital. That's some serious town loyalty right there.

When Mom was a kid, two girls from Calliope went missing while selling Girl Scout cookies in Densdale. Local legend said the girls had been kidnapped by an old woman with a Thin Mint obsession who ate them when she'd finished the cookies. It didn't sound true to me, because I once drank a glass of juice after eating a Thin Mint, and it tasted truly heinous. No way you could eat girls after those cookies.

True or not, convincing Mom to let me go to the movies in Densdale would take skill, or possibly a miracle. Thanks to Robin Goodfellow/Puck the fairy, I had ammunition.

• • •

It was a little-known fact that fairies were the most stubborn creatures in the whole fantastical universe, and my mom was their queen. Luckily, I had almost twelve years' practice in dealing with her.

The house had no toddlers in it when I got home, but they'd been there. A red balloon bobbed on the front porch, and a teeny glitter dust bunny swept past in the breeze. I let myself in and headed straight to the Fairy Wonderland.

If Mom had built her fairy room in anyone else's house,

I might have thought it was pretty cool. Fairy lights sparkled through paper twigs and gauzy leaves on cardboard trees. The carpet was made from the fake-grass stuff people who couldn't be bothered to mow their lawns used. Between the trees were toadstools and giant flowers and rabbits and a shocked-looking baby deer, all made from papier-mâché.

Mom sat right in the middle, cross-legged, on the rock-and-vine party table. She wore her town-pride *Calliopean Cool* T-shirt under her wings, but that wasn't going to put me off.

"You're home early." She gave me her very brightest smile, holding out her arms for a hug.

No such luck, Mother, I thought, and stuck out my chin. "Mrs. Gilbert gave us a new reading assignment today. It's an old play. I can hardly understand the words."

Mom waved her wand in front of her. "Abracadabra, I gift you with extra-super reading skills with which you might ace your assignment, Bob."

I hated it when she called me Bob. My mom was even worse at nicknames than real names.

"Thanks so much," I said.

Even though my mother had a superpowered lie detector built into her brain, it somehow never warned her about sarcasm. She clapped her hands and hopped off the table with a little bounce. "What's the play about?"

"Fairies." No matter how much I narrowed my eyes, she didn't notice.

In fact, she looked kind of like she might explode into a cloud of gauze and glitter. She did a twirl on her tiptoes, clutching her wand. To some people, it might have looked like overkill, but those people didn't know my mom. If she didn't let out her excitement in little bursts, she might go supernova one day.

"I loved studying plays at school." Her eyes always got misty when she rambled on about her theater days in college. For a second, I thought I even saw a tear. "Is it a play I might know?"

By then we were in the kitchen, and Mom was stacking plates of leftover finger sandwiches in the refrigerator, her wand clattering against pickle jars and milk bottles. I felt a bit guilty for being mad at her when she was all soft and dreamy. Then I remembered Robin Goodfellow and got over it. "Oh, I think you've heard of it."

She smiled, a plastic-wrap-covered plate in her hands. "Please tell me it's *Peter Pan*."

"*A Midsummer Night's Dream*."

Her face froze, and her smile sort of dried up. "Oh. I see," she said. All the little dots must have connected inside her brain. "I'd rather you didn't study that play."

"It's too late. I read far enough to know about Puck the fairy, or should I call him Robin Goodfellow?"

"The name? Oh, that's what's bothering you?"

"Of course. The name. What else could it be? Until today, I thought that part of my name was perfectly ordinary."

Her smile looked sort of embarrassed and relieved at the same time. "In my defense, it's taken you nearly twelve years to realize. If it weren't for the assignment, you might never have known. I'll phone Mrs. Gilbert and ask if you can read something else."

What did Mom have against *A Midsummer Night's Dream*? My name couldn't be the problem, since she was the one who'd chosen it, and she had seemed to think there was something else. Fairies, maybe? She knew I got fed up with wings and sparkles sometimes. Most of the time.

"I don't mind studying it, Mom."

"There are other Shakespeare plays that would be much better for you to study." She peeled back the plastic wrap from a plate of sandwiches and held them out. "Fairy bread?"

So inappropriate.

Mom put down the plate and leaned forward to leave a little kiss on the end of my nose, but I didn't smile, even though it was awful hard not to. If I gave in, I wouldn't get to go to Densdale with Nickel that night.

"I have a question. Under the circumstances, I think you should say yes," I said.

"You better let me have it, then." Mom put her hands on her hips, including the hand with her sparkly star wand.

I fluttered my eyelashes and gave her my most adorable smile. "Nickel and I would like to go to the movies in
Densdale tonight. His mom is taking us."

"Densdale? What on earth for?"

"Because Calliope doesn't have a theater . . ."

"No, but there are movies online. I can make popcorn."

My smile stayed firmly in place. "It's not the same. We
want to go to a real theater."

She screwed up her face as if the city were a bad taste
she couldn't get out of her mouth. "I don't know. I mean,
it's Densdale."

"It's only a movie, and Nickel's mom is driving us." I
coughed "Puck" under my breath, to help make my point.

She smiled, which I hoped was a good sign. "You two
aren't running off to get married?"

I rolled my eyes. She knew perfectly well that Nickel
and I were not even boyfriend and girlfriend. Yet. "No,
obviously. But seeing a movie would help me get over the
shock of the whole name thing."

On the spot, Mom shifted and stared down at the floor.
"I guess so, then, against my better judgment. Make sure
your homework's done."

It seemed almost too easy.

CHAPTER 4

I fidgeted in the backseat of Mrs. Bugden's car, wishing I could tell Nickel all about the O'Malleys and talk about the satellite.

"Thanks so much for picking me up," I said. "It's very nice of you, Mrs. Bugden."

Nickel faked a gag in the passenger seat, his freckles bunching up on his nose.

"What are we going to see?"

"*Hounds of Armageddon.* I heard someone talking about it the other day. It sounds a-maz-ing." He wriggled his butt so he could turn around in his seat to look back at me.

"An end-of-the-world movie?" I asked. *With a satellite on its way?*

His smile twitched a bit. "Sure. I mean, it's not just about that, though."

Best friends were worth more than watching bad movies, so I gave him my best smile. "Sounds . . . super."

Nickel's eyebrows shot up, and a grin spread across his face. "We could go to the skate park too if you want."

That was one step too far.

Mrs. Bugden interrupted before I could say anything sarcastic. "Sorry, kids. I'll be back right after. Dad's on evening shift tonight, and I'll need to be home with Penny."

"Aww, man," Nickel said.

"Yeah," I said. "What a shame."

Hounds of Armageddon was everything I had hoped it wouldn't be—bombs, death, explosions, and not a single dog anywhere. I deserved a new belt in Focus Pocus for sitting through the whole thing. We had a series of ten belts, and because earning them required a lot of patience, wisdom, and mind over matter, I had only three. To be honest, two of those were because Nickel felt bad for me. He had all of them.

When the movie was over, we sat on the steps out front and waited for Nickel's mom. Blood-and-guts movies were not good for my appetite. I tossed my uneaten popcorn to the twilight pigeons that cooed at us from the sidewalk below.

"Okay, spit it out," Nickel said, sucking on the dregs of his supersized soda. "I know you're up to something."

Blinking innocently at him, I said, "What gave you that idea?"

From my angle, the bright mall lighting shone right through his hair, turning it pure orange. We had become friends in kindergarten, when we both got teased for our hair—his too red and mine too white. Back then, I should have been popular because of my fairy mother, but the hair ruined most of that. It turned out Nickel could find a hiding place just about anywhere, and I could fast-talk our way out of any situation. Once we invented Focus Pocus and shared our knowledge, we were unbeatable.

Nickel rolled his eyes. "Let me see. First, I know you. Second, you agreed to watch *Hounds of Armageddon* without complaining. Third, you were all, 'Thank you for picking me up, Mrs. Bugden.'" He put on his smarty-pants voice for the last bit.

If I could have found Dad without him, I would have used the Doom Glare.

"Actually, this is very serious stuff," I said.

Nickel's face brightened. "Sweet. What's up?"

I told him that I had found my probable family on TV.

"Wow, that's like some sort of superhero origin story. Like you're an X-Man or something."

That might have been going a bit far. *Hounds of Armageddon* had clearly gotten to him.

"If they are my family, then they must know my dad.

He might have been right there on the TV for all I know. I need to find him."

Nickel grinned. "Need to find him? For what, hockey puck?"

I shoved his arm. "Don't call me that! Dads are useful for all kinds of things. He could sign the papers so I can change my name to something else, for one thing. I can't go to high school with this name. Even worse, if I die from the satellite, I'll be stuck with a fairy's name on my gravestone."

My hands shook as I thought about the satellite. It sat up there in the sky right then, maybe taking aim. I could train in Focus Pocus techniques every day for the rest of my probably shortened life, and I'd still be too slow to get out of the way.

Nickel lifted his brows and shrugged. "If you die by satellite, there probably won't be enough of you left to bury."

My eyes popped wide open. "Nickel Bugden!"

"Okay, okay. Find him, then."

I struggled to turn the ticked-off expression on my face into something a bit more pleading. "I bet you could find him. Easy."

"Me? Oh no, you don't. My dad will kill me if he catches me looking up people in the police database again. He's onto me."

"But this time it's my-own-for-real dad. At least you have a dad to be angry at you."

"Emotional blackmail is the lowest form of negotiating." Nickel rolled his eyes and leaned back on the steps. "The satellite's as likely to hit my house as yours."

"Oh yeah? And how many things have landed on your house? Skydivers? No. Trees?"

He looked a bit less certain and much less sarcastic. "Good point. If it wanted to land on anyone's house, it would definitely choose yours." He gave a pained sigh. "If I get grounded for life, you have to find a way to smuggle me in some candy and soda."

"Deal." I spat on my hand and held it out for him to shake.

He gagged and waved me away.

I pulled my pen from my back pocket and wrote *O'Malley* on his hand. "Thank you!" I leaned over for a hug. He blushed a furious shade of red but didn't try to escape.

Just our luck, Dameon Swenson strutted down the stairs with a group of his friends in time to see the hug. "Aww, you got yourself a Mrs. Ginger, Bugden? You know you two can't breed, right? Your kids will have pink hair."

I reached over, grabbed Nickel's face, and kissed him right on the mouth. His lips were drier than I'd expected, and tight with surprise and panic. My first kiss was supposed to be romantic, but sacrifices had to be made at times like that.

I looked up at Swenson and said, "At least someone will kiss him. I know for a fact every girl in sixth grade swears they'll die of mono before they'll kiss you."

Swenson turned a grape-jelly shade of purple. Nickel turned a similar color himself.

"I'd rather date the older girls in the seventh grade, anyway," Swenson said.

I shook my head. "They all think you're a little puke too."

He muttered something about geeks and wackos and stamped off. His chuckling friends followed a respectful distance behind.

Nickel's face had gone all pale, and he looked like he might hurl. "You kissed me, you weirdo!"

That was a bit rude, but I grinned anyway. "You're welcome."

He took a big swig from his soda cup, swirled it around in his mouth, and spat it into the dried-up strip of garden by the steps. A pigeon let out a noisy protest and flapped out of the way.

"You sure made Swenson look like an idiot, though. It was almost worth it," he said.

I decided to listen to that and forget how he had washed out his mouth. "I've seen Mom deal with jerks like him. The trick is to embarrass them worse than they embarrass you. It only works if you can think of a good comeback, though."

"Next time," Nickel said, tossing his empty soda cup into the trash, "maybe you could try using your words."

One day Nickel would like my kisses just fine. He just wasn't ready to admit it yet, and Swenson had been watching, that was all. Next time I'd let him think kissing was his idea, even though it might take him forever to get around to it.

Oh well, we'd be married when we grew up if I got my way—and I usually did.

Unless the satellite got me first.

● ● ●

It was almost dark by the time Nickel's mom dropped me off at home. I thanked her and waved as they disappeared into the distance. I doubted I'd hear from Nickel before the next day, even if he found anything on the computer. He hated to text, and I'd already used my computer time for the day.

Mrs. Cuthbert stood in her front garden with a dripping hose in her hand. If she planned on watering her garden, it would take a while like that.

"That your boyfriend?" she asked.

Feeling kind of smug, I said, "Yep." Even though it wasn't strictly true.

"I don't approve of dating at your age." She shook her

head. The hose coughed and sputtered and spat out a single plop of water that disappeared into the dry lawn.

I looked at her plaid shorts and orange button-down shirt. This was the woman who had nearly squished me with her giant tree and who spent her days spying on us. I didn't much care what she approved of.

"My mom is proud of everything I do," I said.

"That doesn't surprise me one bit!"

I twirled toward our house and stamped off inside. Mom didn't like plenty of things I did, but she never stopped being proud of me. The details weren't important, though.

If Mrs. Cuthbert didn't approve of me, I had done something right.

CHAPTER 5

I always slept in on Saturdays, but this time I woke up early to the sound of Mom and Mrs. Cuthbert arguing in our front yard. This happened at least once a month, but usually not before Grandma's pancakes filled the house with a smell so happy even a cranky neighbor couldn't ruin the day.

Saturdays meant fairy parties, and often more than one. If I wasn't careful, Mom would have me wearing a tutu and wrangling toddlers. I stayed in my room until I could hear Mom's angry voice in the kitchen as she told Grandma about whatever awful thing Mrs. Cuthbert said this time.

I dressed, put on my hat and sunscreen, and took a paper bag outside to collect the toys that had fallen from the roof with the skydiver. Most of the tennis balls were fine, but anything plastic was faded and brittle from the sun. They still added up to enough to earn a few quarters on the school black market, maybe even a cinnamon bun's worth.

I slipped the last Frisbee into the bag as a car pulled up outside our house. A mother climbed out to unbuckle a squawking toddler from her car seat. Party time. Toddlers were loud and always sticky, but they turned into chubby little balls of human flypaper once they hit the Fairy Wonderland.

I made a run for Robyn Headquarters, a tree house my great-grandpa had built in our backyard for Grandma. Then it became Mom's when she was a kid, and now it was mine. When I inherited it, I redecorated it to hide the flaky old boards and cracks. It had been great until Mrs. Cuthbert decided to get rid of her tree. My headquarters would have been destroyed if the tree had fallen a few inches closer. But it survived, mostly hidden high up in the ancient elm. It was missing a whole wall and could get pretty drafty in winter, though.

There were four rules for Robyn HQ:

1. No birds. (This rule was hard to enforce on account of one missing wall and birds not understanding the meaning of "no trespassers" or "Don't eat my cookies.")
2. No boys. (The only boys who got near were out of their minds from preservatives and food coloring from

fairy parties. They couldn't even see the rope ladder, much less figure out how to use it. I would make an exception for Nickel, but he had a very sensible toddler phobia and never visited my house.)

3. No falling out of, acknowledging, or otherwise encouraging the ginormous hole in the wall.
4. If you hear a chainsaw, forget the rope ladder and jump. Jump for your life.

Hopefully, I would never have to jump. It's hard to out-run a crash-landing satellite or find a father while wearing a plaster body cast.

The rope ladder creaked as I climbed the old elm tree, one careful step at a time. The wooden rungs were getting awful gray and splintery, and the rope had frayed in places. If I found my dad, maybe he could fix my ladder, since Mom and Grandma were always too busy fixing the house to have time for my headquarters. I stopped noticing that the rope felt hard and crackly, and imagined shiny new rungs with rubber grips instead.

Things inside the headquarters were a bit grim. Most of my pictures had blown out of the hole, been torn to bits by the wind, or been carried off to make bird nests. The one proper window still had its little red-and-white-checked curtains, although they were a bit battered.

I opened my notebook on the floor in front of me, took my favorite orange pen from my pocket, and wrote an excellent title with swirly bits at each end to show how important it was.

~My Dad: Pros and Cons~
by Robyn Tinkerbell Goodfellow

Pros:

1. He could help me change my name. Mom chose "Goodfellow" for us when I was little, and she changed our names legally. He could change mine to something else. Robyn O'Malley, for instance.
2. He could tell me where I got my curly hair.
3. He could take me to family get-togethers.
4. He could buy me a pet iguana.

I doodled a picture of an iguana in the margin. What if my dad wasn't interested in helping? He never visited. Never sent birthday cards. He might not know my birthday, but he definitely knew about Christmas and didn't send presents then either. Mom had always lived in our house, so he must have known how to find us if he wanted to. But he never did. Maybe Mom didn't talk about him because he had hurt her feelings too badly.

Cons:

1. He might disagree with owning lizards as pets.
2. He might already have kids. Maybe he was there in the

park and some of those kids were his. He might not even want me. In fact, he already didn't want me, since he wasn't around. Unless Mom never told him. She could be very sneaky.

Mom always said if she could line up every girl in the entire world and choose exactly which one she wanted for her daughter, she would still pick me every time. If that was true, he would be sure to like me. Wouldn't he?

Frowning, I added the last item to the list.

3. He might not care, even if he had the coolest daughter in the world.

I slammed my notebook closed and tucked it into the front of my sweater, scolded a crow perched outside my picture window, and started down the ladder. My foot went straight through the last rung with a loud snap, and I landed hard on the grass with a thud.

Gritting my teeth and rubbing my nose to get rid of the tearful prickles inside it, I got to my feet and half stamped, half limped toward the back door. *Stupid fathers. Stupid ladder.*

I had almost made it when Mrs. Cuthbert's voice stopped me. "Robyn. You're precisely the girl I wanted to see."

Putting my best and sweetest smile on my face, I turned

and gave her a feeble wave in reply. Her head popped up over the top of the fence Grandma had built after Mrs. Cuthbert made it her personal mission to prove we were spies for a corrupt oil baron. The fence did a pretty good job at keeping her out, but I sometimes caught a flash as sunlight hit the glass of her binoculars peering through the knotholes in the wood.

"Hi, Mrs. C."

"Did you hear any wind during the night?" she asked, scratching behind her ear with a clothespin.

I shook my head. Since I had spent half the night tossing and turning, imagining every sound was a satellite speeding to Earth to squash me before I could find my dad or change my name, I would have noticed if there had been any. Wind always whistled around the old house like an orchestra of flutes and violins.

"I didn't hear any either, and yet when I got up this morning"—Mrs. Cuthbert glanced over her shoulder to point at something in her backyard—"all the sheets were gone from my clothesline."

"Grandma says you shouldn't leave your laundry out," I said, "in case it gets stolen."

Mrs. Cuthbert sniffed. "Funny she should say that. Look."

I followed the direction of her pointing finger all the way to the very top of our roof. There, hanging limply from the rooster weather vane, was a sky-blue bedsheet.

"Oh," I said.

"What are you going to do about it?" Mrs. Cuthbert said. "I told that mother of yours this morning that it's time at least one of you people acted like an adult. Since she won't, I guess it will have to be the child who does it."

My throat burned with angry words. I hated when anyone said anything nasty about my mom, because she never said anything nasty about anyone else.

"You lot can't keep collecting things from the neighborhood with that roof of yours. You're kleptomaniacs."

Heat from embarrassment crept up my neck and into my cheeks. Whatever a kleptomaniac was, I didn't think we were it. Although our roof might be. "We have plenty of sheets of our own."

Mrs. Cuthbert's face puckered up. "If you're all so well-off, why doesn't someone fix that disaster of a house?"

I'd never minded the loose boards and flaky paint until she said those words. It stung as if she had insulted me as much as the house.

When I didn't answer, she growled from the other side of the fence. "Someone needs to put a stop to it. Don't go thinking I won't escalate this to a governmental level if I'm pushed. So far, I've hesitated to involve my fellow agents because I believe in being neighborly."

I had to bite my lip to keep my mouth closed when she said that last bit.

Sticking her nose in the air, she said, "You know what people say about your family, don't you?"

Whatever it was, it couldn't be much worse than what they said about Mrs. Cuthbert. The words wouldn't stay inside anymore. "Maybe Grandma could afford to fix up the house if a tree hadn't fallen on it, or if she hadn't had to waste time building a new fence to keep you from spying on us!" I spat out the words and ran inside.

When Grandma found out what I said—and Mrs. Cuthbert would make darn sure she did—I'd be grounded forever.

It kind of seemed worth it.

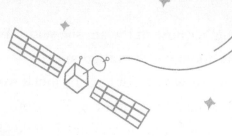

CHAPTER 6

Mrs. Cuthbert had some nerve, arguing with Mom *and* me in a single day.

When I got inside, I leaned against the bookshelf in the hallway to catch my breath and wait for the angry tears to stop burning. A toddler with wide eyes and a cupcake wrapper stuck to her cheek galloped up to me.

"Bathwoom!" she squealed, hopping around in circles.

I backed away and pointed toward the fairy-party bathroom Mom had designed next to the laundry downstairs.

"Fanks!" the kid hollered, running off down the hall and right past the bathroom door.

I hurried up the stairs before she could come back. At least I knew Mom would soon be too busy cleaning up a pee puddle to find some chore for me to do. I tiptoed along the upstairs hall, dodging most of the creaky boards. I had a hand on my bedroom door when Mom stumbled backward out of her room, dragging a suitcase stuffed so full that little pinches of fabric poked out between the zipper teeth.

"Mom?"

She spun around to face me.

"I thought you were outside," she said, running her wrist under her nose. Her eyes were red and swollen, and she sounded like she had a cold. No way. Mom never cried.

"I was, but now I'm inside. Why aren't you downstairs herding toddlers?"

Her eyes went all wide, like I had caught her in the middle of mischief making—which was weird. Normally it was the other way around. "Grandma's giving me a day off. Isn't she sweet?"

People called Grandma a lot of things, but "sweet" didn't come up that often. I almost giggled at the idea of my grandmother in wings and a tutu.

I pointed to the suitcase. "Are you running away from the satellite?"

She glanced down at the bag like it had just appeared out of nowhere. "I got to thinking about some old stuff I've been keeping for much too long. I thought I'd have a spring clean-out."

"It's practically summer."

"Oh, Bob. Don't get technical on me." She grinned and dragged the case on its wobbly wheels toward the stairs.

"I'll help you get it down," I said, mostly so I could take a closer look.

There wasn't much to see. Fabric. Not even any glitter. Whatever treasure Mom had decided to get rid of stayed hidden inside her plaid suitcase.

"What kind of stuff is it?" I asked as we bounced off the last stair.

Mom shrugged, which was when I noticed her wings were missing. "Nothing important." She sniffled. "And dusty. It made me all sneezy."

I didn't buy it, not really. She was up to something, or my name wasn't Robyn Tinkerbell Goodfellow—and unfortunately, it was. The trouble with mysterious mothers was that they'd had more years to practice lying. Mom was excellent at it. I almost believed the dust story. Anyone who had seen inside her room would.

Other people's mothers told their kids to clean their rooms. Not mine. Sometimes I thought about suggesting she organize hers, though. Other people's mothers bought them iguanas, or at least a puppy or a kitten or something, and didn't wear wings. Again, not mine. Although Sarah-Belle Schue's mom sometimes wore cat ears. Other people's moms did lots of things that mine didn't, and mostly I was okay with that—so long as no one was looking.

Right then, Mom looked like any other ordinary mother. Wingless, tutu-less, dragging an old suitcase out to the car. I scurried back up the stairs in case Grandma called me to help with the party or the pee puddle. But what was Mom up to? What did she have in that suitcase that she wouldn't tell me about? There was only one subject she didn't share with me. My dad.

Dad!

He probably wasn't in the suitcase, but clues might be. Dad clues.

I had to stop her.

I raced to the window just in time to see our car disappear down the street.

Great. Stupid, slow brain.

I kicked my bed, then hopped around a bit, rubbing my foot, before chucking my pillow at the wall and knocking down a couple of glow stars. After a few minutes of sitting on my bed, picking at the cover of my notebook, I stopped feeling angry and started feeling hungry instead.

The door downstairs had opened and slammed quite a few times as parents came to collect their kids. That meant there might be leftover birthday cake. I hurried down the stairs, my feet skipping fairy-light over each step.

The hallway was empty.

No toddlers. No parents. No Grandma.

"Hello?" I called out.

"In here." Grandma's voice came from the Fairy Wonderland.

I pushed open the door, and there, looking tired and a bit wilted, stood Grandma. She wore one of Mom's tutus with a pair of slightly crumpled wings on her shoulders. I never saw a worse fairy in all my life.

A giggle bubbled up inside me, and even my best Focus Pocus self-control training could not stop it.

"Don't you laugh, missy. I'm going to need some help cleaning up, and you're the only one available."

The smile slipped off my face. "Me? I have satellites to worry about, and Mom just took off and left me to clean up?"

Grandma laughed. "If we're going to get hit by the satellite, leaving would be a lot smarter than staying."

"Grandma!"

She gave my shoulder a gentle punch. "Hush, I'm kidding."

"The fairy outfit suits you. You should wear it every day," I said as revenge. Grandma's knees were a bit knobbly, and she had to wear a lumpy support bandage around one of them under her tights. Her dark fairy-floss hair looked perfect, though.

She wrinkled her nose and held out her wand like it was a dead mouse. "No way, nohow. First chance I get, I'm hanging up my tutu forever."

As I carried armfuls of used dishes and half-eaten party food into the kitchen, I couldn't help feeling a bit sorry for myself. If the satellite crushed me, I would die fatherless, with a ridiculous name. And I had a bad feeling my mother had just wheeled a suitcase of important clues about my dad out of the house.

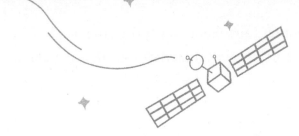

CHAPTER 7

Mom had slept in the same room her whole life. Technically, she wouldn't like me nosing about in there while she was gone. But technically, she was not home to find out, and I needed whatever information might be left after she had taken the suitcase away.

Calling on my Focus Pocus spy training, I eased the door open, taking care not to trip on the spots where the carpet was worn almost through. The room still had things from when Mom was a kid, like faded bits of wallpaper with bunnies on it and the cradle both Mom and I had slept in when we were babies. She kept everything that mattered even the tiniest bit, and I hoped that something of my father would still be there. It looked suspiciously tidy that day, though.

Her bed was buried under a quilt patched together from the same green-and-brown fabric Mom had used for the leaves downstairs. Fairy lights hung over the head of her bed. That was lucky, since the bedroom light had never worked. The closet door had a lock on it, and the key usually poked out of that. But not that day. Tricky mother. Unfortunately, we hadn't added lock picking to our Focus Pocus training program. Not yet, anyway.

The bedside cabinet looked full of possibilities. A silk scarf covered its chipped corners, and I could see an old phone book taking the place of a missing leg. Leaning my shoulder hard against the cabinet, I eased the book from underneath. Its pages were soft and worn, and the date was from when I was two years old. The first third of the pages were missing. Mom had torn them out to make the practice folded fairies that were pressed between the rest of the pages. A few envelopes slipped out and landed on the floor, but I couldn't tell which part of the book they'd been hidden in.

I stuffed them back inside, hoping it wouldn't matter, and hurried to the "O" listings in the middle of the book. Calliope was small, and I knew I was the only kid with albinism in town. I would have noticed a whole family who looked like me. That meant the O'Malley family most likely came from Densdale. There were hundreds of O'Malleys listed in the city, but Mom hadn't underlined or highlighted any of them. I could call every O'Malley in the book, but the numbers probably belonged to other people by now. Even if I found the right O'Malleys, what would I say? "Do you know a man who might have had a daughter with a slightly eccentric fairy impersonator about twelve years ago?"

The whole plan reeked of failure.

I almost had the book back in place when the door swung open.

My head jerked from shock and smacked right into the side of the cabinet with a crack. The cabinet wobbled on its loose leg, and the tub of glittery fairy dust Mom dipped her wand in every morning slipped off the top and spilled all over me.

Grandma cackled and snorted, pointing at me with one hand and holding her belly with the other. "You look the very image of your mother."

Sputtering and choking on the sparkles, I brushed myself off and shoved the phone book back under the cabinet. As it slid in, I heard it connect with something, and a large mason jar decorated in cutouts and glitter rolled out the other side. Grandma frowned, picked it up before I could get a better look, and put it on the dresser. I'd have to wonder about that later. Right then, I had bigger problems.

Most of the glitter was still inside the container, but enough had spilled to be pretty obvious.

"Mom will kill me," I whined.

Grandma wiped a giggle-tear away from the side of her nose. "Naw. She'll be glad she's finally won you over to Team Fairy."

I straightened up. "She did not! Thanks to fairies, I have the stupidest name in history."

Grandma licked her hankie and wiped some of the sparkles off my nose. Fairy names might have been annoying, but I preferred glitter to granny spit on a hankie. "Gross, Grandma!"

She kept right on wiping, moving to my cheeks. "How about you tell me what you were doing in here with the old phone book?"

"Would you believe I was trying to find a satellite-deflector salesperson?"

Grandma shrugged. "Yes. But I'm not sure why you'd bother when you have someone around as handy with a screwdriver as I am."

I had to move the conversation on to safer subjects. "By the way, Mrs. Cuthbert stopped me outside to tell me off. She says we're klepto . . . kepto . . . She was very insulting."

"Kleptomaniacs, are we? Ha." Grandma snorted. "That's practically a compliment, coming from her. Come with me, Sparkles. It's time we taught that lizard-tongued, interfering old biddy a lesson."

• • •

"Here, hold this." Grandma crawled out from under the gigantic camellia bush and passed me the end of the garden hose. I held it between two fingers to keep from touching bugs and dirt. Dusting off her knees, Grandma glanced around to make sure no one could see us.

Crouching down, she hurried across the lawn and waved for me to follow. For a second, I thought she was going to do a Focus Pocus ninja roll behind a bush, but she didn't stop until she reached the fence. I got there a few seconds later, dragging the superlong hose behind me. Grinning, Grandma took it from me, wiped off the nozzle on the end, and twisted it to the setting she wanted. Snorting a little from keeping her giggles quiet, she found a knothole in the wood that was the right size, and she poked the nozzle through.

"Grandma, are you sure this is—"

She put her grubby finger on my lips. "Trust me, little accomplice."

Once it was all set up, we sat together on the back steps in the late-afternoon sunshine.

"Shouldn't you be getting ready for the next party?" I asked, hoping the reminder would send her inside in a panic, far away from Mrs. Cuthbert.

"Nope. It was canceled. We're done for the day."

Grandma was so focused she didn't even look at me as I slapped at the little flying bugs that tickled my ankles. Maybe she wouldn't notice if I hurried back inside to investigate that mason jar in Mom's room.

Mrs. Cuthbert's back door slammed. Her muttering and cussing were loud enough to hear even over the birds squabbling for spots in the shadiest trees.

The smile on Grandma's face made my stomach knot up from nerves. With one hand over her mouth to hold in the chuckles, she tiptoed down the back steps to the tap perched on the side of the house. Counting down from ten, she marked off the numbers with her fingers before twisting the knob around a few times as fast as she could.

All I could do was watch in horror as Grandma's plan came together.

The hose was set to spray, and the heavy mist made a rainbow that hung over the whole of Mrs. Cuthbert's backyard. "My sheets!" she screamed.

"I thought you didn't have any left!" Grandma shouted.

I wanted to run inside, but my feet were glued to the ground.

"Ooh, it's cold, it's cold, turn it off!" Mrs. Cuthbert hollered. Her shrieks reminded me of the argument she'd had with Mom that morning, right before she accused our roof of grand theft laundry.

"Now that they're wet, they'll be too heavy to blow away tonight. You're welcome!" Grandma was on the top step now, stretching to watch Mrs. Cuthbert run for her back door. But it didn't matter to me what that horrible old woman did anymore, not after she'd upset Mom. She could call Officer Bugden or the FBI or the CIA for all I cared.

"I'll fix you, Shirley Cogsworth!" Mrs. Cuthbert hollered from just inside her door.

Grandma held her stomach and kept right on cackling. She took a deep, shaky breath and grinned at me. "Oh, quit looking so worried, Sparkles. There's nothing like a good feud to liven up a neighborhood."

She mistook my smug face for worry.

• • •

Mom arrived home just as we headed inside. Grandma chortled to herself and wiped giggle-tears out of her eyes. Any other day, Mom would have pestered her to find out what was so funny. That day, though, she moaned about being tired and went upstairs to run herself a bath. For her, baths were a major event requiring smelly candles and glittery bath bombs. Honestly, sometimes my mother looked like a Christmas decoration or a vampire, she sparkled so much.

I followed her upstairs, carrying the brush and dustpan so I could pretend to clean up the glitter I'd spilled on her floor if I got caught looking for the mason jar. Sitting on my bed, doing my best to look innocent, I waited while she got her bath things and padded down the hallway to the bathroom. Once the smell of flowers drifted out from under the bathroom door, I knew it was safe.

Sneaking into Mom's room twice in one day was right up there with the naughtiest things I'd ever done to her. I couldn't decide if that made me feel bad or adventurous. A bit of both, I decided.

Except it turned out to be neither.

For the very first time in my whole life, ever, my mother had locked her door. I checked it four or five times to be sure, rattling the handle and giving the door a bit of a kick in case it had gotten stuck. Who knew she even had a key for that rusty old lock?

I was stumped.

I crept down the stairs and into the computer room for an email check before bed. The little blue envelope appeared with a ding. Had Nickel finally had a chance to search for my family on his dad's computer?

Breathing hard, I clicked on the message.

I think I found one of the families. There was an article about their albino kid in the newspaper stories online. I found their address in Dad's database. It's 56 Market Street in Densdale. You owe me, big-time.

Now I had to figure out how to get to Densdale. Again.

CHAPTER 8

By the time I arrived for English on Monday morning, I still hadn't figured out how to get to Densdale. Public transport didn't exist in Calliope, unless you counted old Mr. Bones and his bicycle-powered rickshaw. He was cheap—only a dollar for him to drive you anywhere you liked—but it would take an awful long time to get to Densdale by rickshaw.

"How are we enjoying the play?" Mrs. Gilbert asked, leaning on the edge of her desk and slapping her knees with the book.

Sarah Michaels made a swoony sound and hugged her copy to her chest. She was born to love fairies. In fact, she looked more like one than my mom did, without even trying. She was teeny tiny, with thin little hands, a pointed chin, and enormous eyes. "It's so amazing!"

The rest of us concentrated on making ourselves small to avoid Mrs. Gilbert's calling on us to read a passage.

I sank lower in my seat and squinted my eyes almost closed.

"Excellent. I knew I could count on my favorite class to have good taste," she said. "You will all be pleased to hear that on Saturday afternoon, I'm taking anyone who is interested to see a matinee performance of *A Midsummer Night's Dream* that's playing at the Centurion Theater in Densdale. I know, I know, Densdale. I feel just as bad about it as you do. But this is a perfect opportunity to see the play the way Shakespeare intended." She clapped her hands together in excitement.

Nickel spun around in his seat. His eyes bulged until I thought he might burst some important vein. I widened mine back, although I had no idea what we were trying to say to each other.

He slapped his forehead and hissed at me, "Densdale, duh!"

Suddenly, Shakespeare didn't seem so bad.

• • •

Grandma smelled like apples and cinnamon, which had to be a good sign for dinner. There hadn't been any parties for the day, which meant Mom might be in a helpful mood. I doubted that would make much difference, though. If she didn't want me studying *A Midsummer Night's Dream*, my chances of getting permission to see an actual performance of it were tiny.

Mom crossed her arms and lifted her eyebrows. "Your teacher is taking you to a play about fairies and you actually want to go? On a Saturday?"

That was better than a flat-out no.

I gave her my most honest smile. It kind of hurt my face. I'd practiced a whole speech about how I wanted to give fairies a chance because she loved them so much, but it sounded pretty ridiculous, even in my head. Instead, I said, "Yeah. I'm curious."

Mom turned away from me, chewing on a thumbnail, which would for sure bug her later, since she wanted to grow her nails. Somehow, it seemed weird that she hadn't said no yet. I almost wished she would and get it over with. Almost.

Without saying another word, she scrawled her signature at the bottom of the permission slip, handed it to me, and walked upstairs.

It didn't feel like much of a win.

. . .

At school the next day, all anyone wanted to talk about was the satellite.

In science, Mr. Hicks spoke about it like it was the thrill of a lifetime. "Of course, the probability that the satellite will hit anywhere but the ocean is slim at best."

At best? At worst, maybe.

"Even if it did make landfall, it's unlikely it'd land in our country, much less our state or near any of us."

Joe Minciello's hand shot up. "What sort of damage could it do? Like, will things explode? Giant waves? Dust clouds and stuff?"

Dust clouds? Explosions? I shuddered so hard my pencil rattled on my desk.

Mr. Hicks sat on his desk at the front of the class and rubbed his hands together like Nickel did before eating his favorite burger. "No, no. Nothing that dramatic."

I let some air out.

"I mean, sure, if it landed in a lake, it might make a small wave, I suppose, but not enough to cause any damage. No. We'd only need to worry if it landed in a built-up area. That could cause some major damage or even loss of life."

I held my arm in the air and waved my hand around.

"Robyn?"

"What would it do to an actual house if it hit one? A wooden one, for example?"

"There wouldn't be much left, I imagine. But there's no need to worry. Besides, imagine how cool it'd be to find a piece of the satellite somewhere. I'd give anything for that."

For a teacher, Mr. Hicks was no help at all. The satellite could destroy a house; he'd said so. A house just like our house. With us in it.

Maybe if I found Dad, he'd let Grandma, Mom, and me stay at his place till the satellite crisis was over.

That evening, I took *A Midsummer Night's Dream* and my notebook up into Robyn HQ. My notebook had a few more entries in it by then. I had the possible O'Malley address and a plan to meet them. Once we were together, they would tell me how to find my dad, and everything else would fall into place.

Shivering even though it was warm outside, I slammed my notebook closed and opened *A Midsummer Night's Dream*. For once, it seemed like a good distraction. Everyone else would get to watch the performance on Saturday, but Nickel and I would sneak out to find the O'Malleys as soon as the curtain went up. Either I figured out the play on my own, or I would end up looking stupider than Dameon Swenson when Mrs. Gilbert discussed it on Monday.

A crow sat in the hole where my headquarters' wall used to be. It cocked its head to the side, listening while I read the words aloud. " 'How now, spirit! Whither wander you?' "

The crow looked quite impressed and let out a caw of approval.

"But what does it mean?" I asked.

The crow didn't know or wasn't telling. It hopped around a bit before settling down again to watch. Such a willing audience deserved a show. I got up on my knees and waved one arm in the air.

" 'How now, spirit! Whither' "—wave, wave—" 'wander you?' "

The crow cawed again and flapped its wings. I dipped into a low bow, which was what you did when asked for an encore. It made me feel smarter, saying the words out loud, even if I wasn't sure yet what they meant.

" 'The king doth keep his revels here tonight. Take heed the queen come not within his sight.' " I looked at the bird. "Do you understand this stuff, crow?" The crow bobbed up and down a bit, which must have been the bird's version of a nod.

"Shakespeare, you win this round," I muttered. The crow let out an offended caw and flapped away.

I closed the book, tucked it into the back of my jeans, and scurried down the ladder. More bits of the rope were fraying. At that rate, Robyn HQ might kill me before the satellite had a chance.

• • •

Right after the news headlines, they played a story about the satellite.

"NASA now predicts XR-26 is most likely to land somewhere in the Northern Hemisphere, with a fifty percent chance of making landfall."

They should have talked to me. My prediction was way more accurate than 50 percent. Heck, I could give them our address and permission for a news crew to film it live.

I got up and hugged Mom and Grandma good night. "I'm tired," I lied.

"Night night, sweetie." Mom beamed her usual big smile at me, which made me feel a lot better, because she was still my always Mom.

Grandma yawned and rubbed her eyes behind her reading glasses. "By the way, be careful when you go into the upstairs bathroom."

Aside from a bit of mold over the winter, our bathroom had never been dangerous before. "Why?"

"A softball shattered the window earlier, and a squirrel has moved in."

There weren't any kids in our neighborhood who played softball or any adults who were lively enough. Nickel told me windows never broke at his house, but it sure happened to us a lot. Mom and Grandma even had an account with the glass-repair place. I guessed that was what happened when your roof attracted foreign objects.

Sure enough, when I opened the bathroom door and switched on the light, a pair of beady eyes peered back at me from the top of the shower curtain rod.

Animal, toy, or satellite: sooner or later everything hit our house.

I couldn't use the bathroom with a bushy-tailed rodent staring at me, so I hurried back downstairs to use the party toilet. Mom and Grandma were talking in quiet voices in the kitchen when I passed. I stopped outside the doorway to listen.

"Bah. Don't worry so much. It might never happen," Grandma said.

Mom sighed. "It's going to happen—they're pretty clear about that. The question is where. What if Robyn's right to be scared? Things do seem to end up on our roof. It's not impossible."

The possibility of being right had never felt so wrong.

It was quiet for a minute, and I stretched out my earlobes to let more sound in.

Grandma sighed. "No way to tell, far as I can see, till it happens. So we hunker down, keep an eye on the news, and don't scare Robyn in the meantime."

Too late—I was already scared. Plus, they'd called me Robyn. No nicknames. That meant things were serious. I needed the bathroom more than ever now.

● ● ●

At lunch the next day, Nickel quit poking at his food and stared at me. He wore the most confused look I'd ever seen on anyone, including little kids with too much food coloring in their systems. "You want me to do what?"

"Apply for Space Camp, duh. Is it that hard to understand?" I asked.

Honestly, it was like he didn't even try to use his imagination sometimes.

"Yeah, it kind of is." He rubbed his eyes like he had just woken up, and blinked at me. "I hate space. It's all . . . spacey, and there's possible UFOs and black holes and other horrible stuff. There's absolutely nothing between us and getting sucked into a space vacuum."

"Except the atmosphere!"

He shook his head. "No way am I going to Space Camp. I'm happy on this planet, thank you very much."

"It's on Earth, silly. They don't have UFOs on Earth, most of the time. And you couldn't fit a black hole in NASA, I'm pretty sure." Sometimes I had to explain everything for him. It had something to do with boy hormones; they made him a bit dense sometimes.

"But I don't want to. And I mean I *really* do not want to." He said it like it would make any difference.

"Not even for me?"

He shook his head. "Not even for you."

"But, Nickel, if you go to Space Camp, you can tell NASA how their satellite is going to land on my house and make them put up some sort of satellite-repelling force field. Something like that. They're NASA; they'll know what to do." When I said those words, it made my tummy get all tied into the sort of knots that never came undone. Trying not to sound too desperate, I added, "Please."

Groaning, he leaned forward until his forehead rested on the lunch table between his droopy salad and his most-likely-meat-loaf. I reached past his cup of soda and patted his head. His hair was all rough, like the hair on his terrier, Whiskits. Nickel had wanted to call him Whiskers, and his little sister, Penny, had wanted to call him Biscuit—so it ended up as Whiskits.

"It's life or death, and there is no other possible way for us to make NASA understand. None. I have thought of everything," I said.

Nickel looked up at me. "I could email them."

I lifted my eyebrows. "Or that."

CHAPTER 9

Nickel emailed NASA to explain my problems, and that night, he sent me a copy. He could write like Shakespeare, but in regular English. Maybe he'd write movies or presidential speeches one day. I bet he could if he wanted to.

Dear NASA,

As you are aware, your satellite called XR-26 is planning to come down soon and crash either into the ocean or on land. My friend, named Robyn after a famous fairy, says it's going to land on her house, which she doesn't like the idea of. We know this is true because everything lands on Robyn's house.

Can you please tell Robyn how to protect her house the best way? Or come and fix it yourself. It's kind of your job because it's your satellite and you shouldn't

have it landing on people's houses. It's pretty irresponsible.

Yours faithfully,
Mr. N. Bugden

I held my hands to my chest and sighed.

Good old Nickel. I especially liked the bit about how it was their job to fix things. After all, they wouldn't want to be sued. Although it is a bit hard to sue after you've been squashed by a satellite that plummeted to Earth and exploded into a fireball, taking you and your whole house with it.

"Bedtime, Bob!" Mom called from the kitchen. I closed down my email and slumped upstairs.

Unlike most people in Calliope, Mom and I never went to church. Mostly, I didn't mind. But it seemed to me that with a satellite heading for my house and a recently discovered potential dad, it couldn't hurt to get a bit of religion into my life.

I put on my pajamas and knelt on the floor beside my bed with my hands in the prayer position.

"Dear God." I squeezed my palms and fingers together as tight as I could so God would see I meant business. "Please don't let the satellite land on my house, or anyone else's. Try the ocean, but don't hit any whales, because they're endangered and have enough problems." I thought hard for a second to make sure I wouldn't forget anything.

"Please help me find my dad and make him happy to see me. And maybe make my mom happy to see him too. Amen."

I figured I'd better stop there. It was best not to give God too much to do all at once. There were probably a few other kids with requests.

Later, when my stars ran out of glow and the dark crept into all the corners of my room, I caught a glimpse of the real stars through my window. They didn't seem so beautiful anymore. For all I knew, most of them were satellites hovering around, waiting for their chance to squish me.

• • •

Nickel checked his email every morning before school and at least twice after, but we hadn't heard anything by the weekend. We would have to go ahead with our plan during the play.

The school bus had no air-conditioning. Half the windows were jammed shut, and everyone was cranky. I felt like a sardine squashed into a giant yellow tin can. Worst of all, we were trapped inside a moving vehicle with Dameon Swenson. At least we were headed to Densdale. If it hadn't been for that, I'd probably have faked car sickness.

"Aw, look at little Mr. and Mrs. Pink all snuggled up together," Swenson said, sniggering from the seat behind us.

I opened my mouth to say something in return, but

Nickel elbowed me. "If you kiss me right now, I'll have to transfer to a school in Densdale, because it won't just be Swenson torturing me."

"I wasn't going to kiss you. Sheesh. I have better things to do with my lips."

I didn't really, but my lips still had some pride. I folded my arms tight against my chest and thought the most furious thoughts I could come up with. I very nearly, but not quite, wished XR-26 would land on Swenson's house. But wishing a satellite would land on someone else was the surest way to have it land on you. Karma did things like that to keep you honest.

Mrs. Gilbert stood in the middle of the bus and conducted while we sang a countdown from ninety-nine bottles. Everybody joined in. Swenson opened his mouth to make another sarcastic comment, but no one could hear it. Frowning, he gave up and moved his lips along with the words.

Nickel whispered right into my ear. "What's our plan?"

I tried to answer, but if I talked loud enough for him to hear, everyone else would hear as well. Planning would have to wait until we were inside.

We still had thirty-four bottles left on the wall when the bus pulled up outside the Centurion Theater. My smile stuck to my face like I had used superglue on it. This was it. Today was the day I would find my other family. I took a deep breath and looked around.

Before we left our seats, Mrs. Gilbert stood up at the front of the bus. "Now listen very carefully. I expect you all to be good ambassadors today, for our school and for Calliope. This is Densdale, so I need you to stick together, and no one is to wander off alone. Do I make myself clear?"

Technically, when Nickel and I wandered off, it would be together and not alone. So I chanted along with everyone else, "Yes, Mrs. Gilbert."

The street didn't have many cars on it. I needed the place to be busy enough that no one would notice two kids on their own. Lucky for me, cars had arrived by the time we all lined up, ready to file past the box office.

"How are we going to get out of here?" Nickel whispered to me as we waited in line. "And how exactly are we going to get to Market Street?"

I lifted my finger to my lips to hush him. "I'll tell you when the time comes. Relax."

He would be so impressed when he heard the whole plan, because it was epic and guaranteed to succeed. It included such highlights as excusing ourselves to use the bathroom, sneaking outside, and doing a Focus Pocus ninja roll right past the box office. After that, all we had to do was find a bus stop, which had to be easy in a big city like Densdale, and ask the driver to take us to Market Street. Foolproof.

Mrs. Gilbert hurried us all inside and to our seats. Our group got the whole balcony to itself, which gave us a great view of the stage. Nickel and I were put right at the front, which would make it much harder to sneak out. He leaned over the barrier to check out the filled seats below.

He waved at me to join him. "Come look at this. You can see all the way down."

"No, you come here," I growled. We had plans to discuss.

"Just for once, could you listen to me?" he asked.

"Eventually, maybe."

By the time he gave up glaring at me and sat beside me, there were candy wrappers and spitballs and who knew what else being fired from the back rows. I could feel something stuck to my ponytail but didn't dare feel to see what it was. Gross.

Mrs. Gilbert stood up in the middle of the rows.

"That is enough! We are representatives of our school, and you are all making a dreadful impression. Sit down right now!" Her voice got all high and squeaky, the way it did when detentions were about to be dished out willy-nilly.

She stalked up and down the rows, taking away food and paper-related missiles. Finally, she moved Swenson and his friends to the front row. No one had the nerve to fire things at them, which stopped the missiles, but the move put them close enough to harass Nickel and me.

We wriggled ourselves as far down in our seats as we could.

Now that it was quieter upstairs, the noise from downstairs filled every corner. A group of kids in the seats below was making so much noise that we sounded like well-behaved sweetie pies by comparison. That was quite an achievement, considering we had Swenson in our class.

The lights in the theater lowered, and the ones on the stage got brighter as the curtain went up. The kids downstairs didn't get quieter when the play started, even with their mothers hissing and snarling at them. Onstage someone had built a fairy wonderland, which reminded me of ours but was not quite as well done. A little bubble of pride in Mom's talent burst in my chest.

When the professional-type actors recited Shakespeare, a strange thing happened. Maybe it was seeing the action along with the words, but it almost made sense. It was funny too, especially Puck. If only he hadn't been a fairy, my name might not have been so bad after all.

Halfway through the first scene, Nickel and I bent over and tiptoed out of our seats to find Mrs. Gilbert.

"We're both desperate for the bathroom," Nickel whispered to her.

She gave us her "well, isn't that a coincidence?" face but let us go. Because what teacher wants a pair of kids to wet their pants in the middle of a public theater?

We crept down the balcony stairs, which were wide, carpeted in musty red, and lit only by rows of lights near the floor. Nickel's face looked pretty spooky with lights shining on it from that angle.

"You look like Frankenstein," I said.

He lifted his hands and made a strangled roaring sound at me. It would have worked better if he hadn't needed to whisper.

Downstairs, our plan came to a grinding halt. Some guy in a fancy-looking uniform with a tall hat stood, arms folded, in front of the door. One look at him and my nerve sank to the toes of my shoes. There had to be a law against that sort of thing—holding an entire theater full of kids hostage.

"Bathroom is that way," he said, pointing to a set of doors at the side of the lobby.

My stomach gurgled at the cranky way he peered down his long nose at us. Now I needed the bathroom for real. We trudged through the doors and down a long, shadowy hallway.

"Maybe there's an open window in one of them," Nickel whispered.

The light blinded me when I walked into the ladies' room. Because the guy guarding the front door was all dressed up, I expected the bathrooms to be grand too, but no such luck. If anyone had cleaned them recently, they had forgotten about adding more toilet paper to the stalls and soap to the dispensers.

I checked every stall and every wall, but there weren't

any windows, much less any open ones. Hopefully, Nickel's luck had been better.

When I got back into the hallway, it was empty. Nickel still had not appeared two minutes later. I slid down the wall to sit on the floor, trying very hard to be patient.

I counted the seconds until they added up to another two entire minutes. Maybe Nickel had decided to go back to our seats without me. Or perhaps he had found an open window and forgotten to wait for me before climbing outside, and he couldn't get back in through the locked and guarded doors.

After another three minutes and fifty-five seconds, I got back to my feet. Clearly my future husband had escaped or deserted me, or was suffering from the worst case of the runs known to man. Or . . .

Nickel had told me Swenson had threatened to flush his head right down the toilet one day. Maybe Swenson had chosen that moment to strike. Maybe right then, poor Nickel was up to his eyeballs in truly heinous toilet water, with Swenson cackling like a hyena.

No Focus Pocus master could allow a comrade to go in such a humiliating and gross way. I had to take action.

Mustering all the nerve I could find, I put my hand on the door of the boys' bathroom. Going inside would feel all wrong, like accidentally-on-purpose walking into the teachers' staff room, or meeting Dr. Marston in the supermarket without his stethoscope and lab coat.

At first I couldn't see a thing. The boys' bathroom was even brighter than the girls' one. Blinking and squinting, I waited for my eyes to adjust.

When they did, I could not believe what I saw.

Nickel. Standing at the sinks with a boy. A boy with very white, extremely curly hair.

CHAPTER 10

The boy with white hair ignored me and squinted at his phone, like it was no big deal to have a girl in the boys' bathroom, and kept talking.

Nickel threw his hands up in the air. "What the heck, Robyn? You can't come in here."

"I sat out there in the hallway forever, so I can come in. It's like . . . a rule. If you have to wait more than five minutes, all bets are off." I turned in circles, checking out the bathroom. I might never get another chance.

Not only was it clean, but it had extra toilets mounted on the wall for boys to pee standing up. They even had little round cakes of soap in the bottom for the boys to use as targets—which made sense. Anyone who saw our downstairs bathroom after a party with boy guests knew males were not born with natural aim.

Like in the girls' bathroom, there wasn't a single window anywhere.

"You made that rule up," the white-haired boy said. He looked a little older than us. Thirteen, maybe. Fourteen at most.

"She always does. You get used to it," Nickel said.

I opened my mouth to speak, but nothing came out except a huff of air.

"It was supposed to be a surprise." Nickel did one of his big floppy sighs.

"Surprise me, then." I started to cover my face with my hands before I remembered all the bacteria on them. This bathroom had plenty of paper towels, and the dispensers were full of soap. They probably never got used up because boys didn't wash their hands without someone nagging them to do it.

With an impatient look on his face, Nickel waited for me to finish washing my hands. Once I'd dried them, he said, "This is Michael. He is—"

"An O'Malley?" I asked. The hair and the pale skin and eyes, plus me not being a complete nincompoop, made it easy to figure out.

Michael tilted his head to the side and looked at me out of the corner of his eye. "You do look like you're part of the family."

Family. I liked that word. It made my insides ache in a good way. Not that Mom and Grandma and me weren't a family, but we were a pretty small one. I felt taller after he said that, bigger, like instead of being a little pinhole on the map of humanity, I was a whole pushpin.

Finding one of my possible cousins was great, but what I really needed was to find my father. I had to get to the point. "Do you think my dad could be one of your family?" I asked.

Michael shrugged. Even though I could be a relative of his—even a long-lost sister, for all he knew—he ignored me and turned back to Nickel. "What happened next?"

I waved my hands at them to make sure I hadn't turned invisible.

Nickel lifted his butt onto the counter between two sinks. "Where were we up to?"

"The middle of the battle. That dude threw the grenade and then realized he'd forgotten to pull the pin," Michael said.

"*Hounds of Armageddon*? You're talking about a movie?" Sometimes I wondered what the point of boys even was.

Michael yawned at me. "What? You're still here?"

My jaw hit my chest. I could barely even see through all my blinking. "I'm most probably your relative, you know. I mean, that's a big deal. I mean . . . I mean . . . I—"

Michael pulled a sneery face at me. "I have three older sisters, and like a dozen cousins, and they're nothing but pains in the butt. You'd just be another one."

Fists clenched at my sides, I stamped out. I tried to slam the door, but it had one of those automatic closer things, so it wouldn't slam. I grabbed it and pulled it hard, but it stubbornly eased itself shut.

"Argh!" I stomped off and thumped my fist into the hallway wall instead. A shock of pain shot up my arm. I hugged my hand and bit my lip hard.

Eyes watering, I counted thirty seconds. No matter how hard I stared at it, the door of the boys' bathroom didn't open, and Nickel didn't come out to apologize. Our future marriage and our entire friendship were in serious danger.

The thing about fighting with my best friend/eventual husband was that it made it hard to tiptoe back to my seat with dignity. I was stuck in the stupid theater, and my accomplice had changed teams.

When I found my seat in the dark, I slumped down into it. While half watching the play, I counted all the ways I knew to embarrass Nickel. There sure were a lot of them. We'd been friends practically an eternity. But the trouble with thinking about that was remembering all the fun things we had done together. Like the time Nickel bought us lime-berry shakes from Hannah's Shakin' Shack when they were about to close for the day. Hannah gave us extra ice cream, syrup, and sprinkles in our shakes, for free.

And then there was all the time we'd spent inventing Focus Pocus and Doom Glares and planning to outsmart

Swenson and every other enemy we went up against. Together. His spy skills and my fast-talking. It was only good because we did it together. Apart, we were just a sneak and a chatterbox.

My nose got all prickly and my eyes stung. Having a new family was not at all like I had imagined.

Nickel came back eventually and slipped into his seat beside me. I hadn't counted the minutes he'd been gone. It didn't matter. I was ten past ticked already.

"Sorry," he whispered in my ear.

I shoved my hands into my armpits, because (a) it made me look almost as angry as I felt, and (b) it kept me from poking him.

Nickel stared at the play like it interested him, until the curtain closed.

"Phew, it's over," someone said in the back seats.

"I beg your pardon?" Mrs. Gilbert said. "And actually, it's only intermission. It will start again in ten minutes." She stood up as the lights came on one at a time. "Now is the time for a bathroom break, if you need it." She stared straight at Nickel and me. "Or need it again. Otherwise, stay put. And don't even think about going outside."

Sagging, I covered my face with my hands. Would the day ever end?

Nickel poked at my arm. "You're mad at me, right?"

I lifted my nose high enough for me to see all the carved bits and domes in the ceiling.

"I'm going to go right ahead and take that as a yes," he said.

Since I couldn't get my nose any higher, I turned my head a little bit to the left, away from Nickel. I gave myself enough room to keep turning if he kept on talking.

"That kid was a jerk. A total certifiable lame-o."

Turn.

"I didn't like him either. Even if he did like *Hounds of Armageddon*."

Turn. Although my neck ached from the stretch.

"He's totally bored with the whole albinism-slash-family thing."

I jerked and twisted my head around until it stung. Unless I turned into an owl, I'd gone as far as I could without dislocating something.

"Aw, c'mon, listen to me. We talked about the movie, and other stuff came out. I found out loads."

Hoping it wouldn't look too much like forgiveness, I turned my head back toward him, just a little. My neck ached, but I refused to rub it. That would be a sign of weakness—and poor posture.

On the right track now, Nickel kept going. "I'll prove it. Look over the edge of the balcony."

He took my hand, but I snatched it back. "Too soon," I said.

We stood and leaned over to watch the people taking their seats below after their bathroom break. I didn't need

Nickel to tell me what to look for. Right below us sat a small group of moms and their kids—all with ghostly-pale springy hair like Michael and I had. There were not as many of them as there had been at Towne Park, but there were plenty enough to not be a coincidence. They were laughing and play wrestling and fist-bumping, having a great time and making a lot of noise.

"My family?" I asked.

My family!

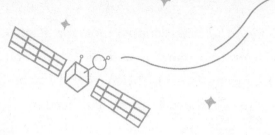

CHAPTER 11

Nickel was officially forgiven.

By some miracle, he'd managed to find an entire theater packed with people related to me. Maybe including some brothers and sisters. It didn't even matter that we had failed in our escape plan, although I was a little disappointed that I wouldn't get to use my Focus Pocus ninja rolls.

I thumped Nickel's arm and pointed at the group in the seats below us. "Wow. Look."

"Ow. I am looking. I showed you, remember," he said.

"Ha!" said Joe Minciello, one of Swenson's friends. "You should get down there. It's like a convention or something. You might even fit in somewhere for a change."

It was much better than a convention—it was a mini family gathering. My family. They were people like me, and no one had ever been like me.

Thanks to the noise Minciello made, Mrs. Gilbert noticed us leaning over the balcony. She rushed down the steps, grabbed Nickel and me by our arms, and pulled us back into our seats. "Get away from there! You'll fall and your parents will sue me."

"Sorry." Nickel slumped into his seat with a sheepish look on his face.

Mrs. Gilbert patted us both on top of our heads. She pointed a warning finger at Minciello and Swenson. "Stay in your seats. All of you."

When she had gone, Nickel swiped his hand across his brow. "Phew."

"That was fun," I said. Which it wasn't.

"You know what this means, right?" Nickel asked.

"Sure, I do," I said. My new family was downstairs waiting for me; that was what.

Michael had been a disappointment. He had rubbed some of the fairy dust off the excitement of finding them, but I couldn't let one bad Michael ruin the entire family. Besides, what mattered was finding my father, and my chance was slipping away.

"I wish I'd read the play properly," I whispered in Nickel's ear.

"Why?"

"Because I'd know when it was ending, so we could be ready to get downstairs fast."

"I'll tell you when it's about to end."

"You read the book?" I asked. Usually I did the reading and gave him a rundown on it.

Even in the dark, I could see his cheeks turn pink. "Yeah. I, uh, kind of liked it."

Sometimes it was like I did not know Nickel at all.

The noisy group downstairs, my O'Malley family, made it hard to hear the play. I closed my eyes and thought about what I might do when I met my father.

I wouldn't show him my list straight off. That might scare him away, and the satellite was the urgent thing. We could start by getting ice cream. That was the sort of thing a father and daughter did. Once we got to know each other, he could come and see Mom and—

Nickel shoved my shoulder. "This is the last scene," he whispered.

A little buzz started up in my stomach. "Okay. Soon as the curtain drops, we make a run for the stairs."

Nickel nodded. "What about Mrs. Gilbert?"

"If we run fast enough, she won't have time to stop us. We have to talk to them before they get a chance to leave."

The spotlights on the stage dimmed for a second, and I jumped up. Nickel dragged me back down again. "Not yet."

A few minutes passed, but it felt way longer than that. One of the actors said something that must have been funny, and everyone laughed and clapped. I jumped to my feet. Nickel stopped me again.

After the next round of applause, I hesitated, not wanting to make a total goose of myself three times in a row.

Nickel jumped up and dragged me with him as the curtain fell for real. I guess all the upping and downing had alerted Mrs. Gilbert, because when we got to the stairs, she was already there.

"Where are you two going?"

Nickel stepped forward. "It's Robyn," he said, thrusting a finger in my direction. "She's got the squirts. The runs. Bad. Terminal, maybe." That boy had a mind as quick as a toddler with a sugar rush.

One of Mrs. Gilbert's eyebrows lifted. "That doesn't take two of you, now, does it?"

Nickel looked at me. He had on his taking-one-for-the-team face. "I'll wait."

He saluted me, and I took off running.

At the bottom of the stairs, I realized that the few-second delay had cost me. My path was blocked by a solid wall of people, all pushing to be the next through the door. My family must have sprinted out of the theater, because most of them were already outside, including Michael. He had one of the others' heads under his arm and was rubbing his fist in the poor kid's hair. Michael had gotten the bad genes. No doubt about it.

I dove for a gap between two old ladies, but it got me no closer to the door. Elbows jabbed me and bodies jostled me until I was right back where I had started.

A hand shot out of nowhere and grabbed my arm. A woman had me trapped—a woman with a wild-eyed look and hair that had more trouble staying in its ponytail than mine did. My mouth did that opening-and-shutting thing fish mouths do when a cat flicks them out of their bowl.

"Where do you think you're going, young lady? We said to wait inside. Is that so difficult to understand? Almost getting us all kicked out of the matinee wasn't enough for you lot?"

"I—but—I didn't—I'm . . ." My plan hadn't allowed for being caught by a raving-mad mother. I needed to improvise a way out of this, and for once my Focus Pocus quick thinking wasn't helping at all. "M-my name is Robyn Goodfellow, and—"

"Oh, I bet it is," the woman said. "Nasty, mischievous fairy, are you?"

Mom had called me that a time or two. But this time, aside from a bit of lying about deadly diarrhea, I wasn't being nasty, and I was mostly failing at being mischievous. "No. I'm Robyn Goodfellow for absolute real. I—"

Her grip on my arm tightened. A lot. I considered hollering for the fancy door guy to come and rescue me. Or Nickel.

"When we say 'stay inside,' we mean 'stay inside.' Now, you freeze right—"

Another one of the mothers interrupted her, pointing at my face. "Take a good look, Nora. Ignoring the hair and the eyes, does this face look familiar?"

Nora peered at me, eyes getting narrower by the second. "Um . . ."

I cleared my throat. "My name is for real Robyn Goodfellow. I'm not a fairy, although my mom is, kind of. I came here with my teacher, but I think my dad is one of your family, and you had a picnic in Calliope that one time. I have to find my father. It's life or death."

The words came out in a terrible rush, but I had more than the two mothers listening by the time I finished. I had another four. I looked from one mother's face to the next, hoping for some sympathy. They all looked confused, and one or two of them looked worried.

"Please." I glanced up at the top of the stairs, where Mrs. Gilbert was shouting orders at everyone. "I don't have much time. Can any of you help me?"

Outside, the kid Michael had in a headlock let out a bellow as his glasses hit the pavement. One of the mothers elbowed her way past while the others looked at me with curious eyes.

The one helpful mother pulled a piece of paper from her pocket, scribbled on it with a chewed-on pencil, and passed it to me. "We have to go. Come to our next get-together. Maybe we can help you figure this out."

Clutching the slip of paper, I watched her disappear into the crowd to join my possible family.

I didn't notice Mrs. Gilbert and the others making

their way down the stairs. Suddenly, they were right there with me.

"Is your tummy okay?" Mrs. Gilbert asked.

I nodded and slipped my hand with the note in it into my pocket. "Yeah. Better now."

Swenson passed by, chuckling to himself. When he reached the doors, he did a squeaky imitation of Mrs. Gilbert's voice and shoved Minciello's arm. "Aww, Minci, you got a runny tum-tum too?"

Fury bunched my hands into tight fists. One day karma would catch up with Swenson, and it would be epic.

Mrs. Gilbert herded us all onto the bus.

My fist had gotten a bit gross and sweaty in my pocket, but I didn't dare pull the paper out, even to show Nickel. What if Mrs. Gilbert saw it and confiscated it, and I couldn't find out what it said until the next issue of the school paper?

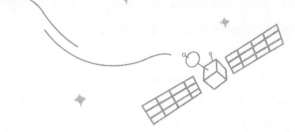

CHAPTER 12

On the bus ride home from the theater, Mrs. Gilbert stood in the aisle right in front of Nickel and me and continued the bottles-on-the-wall countdown at thirty-four. It seemed like I would never get to read my note.

Nickel never had been any good at being patient. "Did you talk to Michael's family?"

"Yeah. I got a note."

"That's something, I guess. What's the note say?"

"I'm not sure yet." I told him in a whisper about the worn-out-looking mothers, about Michael being a jerk, and about the mom who had tried to help me.

"Maybe the note has someone's phone number on it," he said.

It didn't feel like a number, there in my pocket. It felt kind of like soggy paper.

Nickel's eyes got all bright. Sometimes with him you could actually see his imagination kick in. "Maybe it's your dad's phone number, with some secret code only his kids get to use when they call."

I gave him a look. "Secret code? Seriously?"

He shrugged. "You can't say for sure it isn't."

When we got back to school, Mrs. Bugden's car pulled up first. Nickel cursed and muttered all the way out of the bus about efficient mothers. "Email me," he said before slamming the car door behind him.

I waved with my free hand and waited for Grandma while Mrs. Gilbert supervised all the kids going home with their moms.

Maybe the day's party would be over and Mom would pick me up for once instead of Grandma. I kind of missed her after dealing with those other mothers at the theater. Sure, my mother wore fairy wings, but she never snarled or grabbed anyone by the arm, even when toddlers had complete meltdowns. No one ever had a better mother than her.

I thought of Michael and the poor kid he'd had in a headlock. I bet Michael belonged to that cranky mom.

Soon the street outside school was empty of cars, but there was still no sign of Grandma.

Mrs. Gilbert pointed at her cute little car. "How about I give you a ride home? Your grandma must have been busy."

"Busy" was a nice way of saying "You've been forgotten, or maybe abandoned."

Mrs. Gilbert nodded sympathetically. A woman who had Dameon Swenson in her class would understand better than anyone the sort of trouble kids could be.

Mom glanced at the floor with shifty eyes. "How was the play?"

"It went well, I think," said Mrs. Gilbert. "At least our kids weren't the worst behaved in the theater."

Grandma plopped the clothes onto the party table to add to the lost-and-found box if no one came back for them. "Why don't you give Mrs. Gilbert the grand tour, Robyn? The fire department is on their way, and I have to go outside to defend my roses. There's another cat on the roof."

Calliope's cats spent a lot of time on our roof, even though the house was three floors high if you included the attic. No one knew how they got up there, but they did it often enough for the fire department to develop a standard Goodfellow Cat Rescue Plan, or GCRP.

Mrs. Gilbert clasped her hands. "A tour?"

"Okay, then. I guess." I waved my arms a bit, making vague pointing motions at various things in the room. "There's not much to show. Only this."

Mrs. Gilbert smiled. "It's magical."

I realized it had been ages since I'd let myself really look at that room. I thought of the hours Mom had spent sitting cross-legged on the floor, painting the shadows and highlights on the bark until it looked like you could graze your knuckles on it.

I wrapped my arms around the warm feeling in my middle. "It kind of *is* magical."

. . .

As soon as I closed the front door behind Mrs. Gilbert, I ran out back, clambered up the rope ladder, and spread the smeared note on the floor of my headquarters.

Family get-together next Saturday afternoon at the Densdale Lagoon. We'll talk about my brother, Benjamin. Hope to see you then.

Alyssa

Every single word burned itself into my brain. I folded the note neatly and hid it under a big stone in the farthest corner of my headquarters. My heart flipped around with excitement until it made my head go all swimmy. Benjamin? Was that my dad's name? Benjamin O'Malley?

One week, and I would know about my father. Even if he didn't want me, even if all I could get out of him was a signature on a name-change form, it would be enough. Maybe.

Focus Pocus had taught me to concentrate on things I could do instead of things that might go wrong. Planning. That was what I needed. I hurried inside and emailed the note contents to Nickel so we'd have two brains working on the problem.

Mom had promised me a million times she would take me to the Densdale Lagoon. It wasn't a real lagoon, although someone had gone to a lot of trouble to make it look like one. It was a water park with rides and slides and lazy rivers and real waves you could surf on if you were brave enough.

Whenever we made plans, someone would book a last-minute party, or some long-lost college friend would come to town.

"Sorry, Bob," Mom would say. "Next time, maybe. There's nothing that special there, anyway. We're better off safe at home."

So we never actually went. Nothing in Densdale that Mom promised ever happened. And now I was back where I'd started—needing to find a way to get there. Again.

• • •

On Sunday evening, Grandma and I sat together on the sofa to watch the news. She'd won the coin toss and got to sit on the comfortable end. I wriggled around, trying to avoid the poky spring.

The news anchor gave us the latest satellite report while wearing a grim expression.

"I'd feel a lot better if they knew exactly where it would land." I shivered, as if it were the middle of winter instead of the end of spring. Grandma pulled me closer, and I snuggled under her arm.

"Oh, Sparkles, don't panic. The chances of it landing on our house are teeny. Maybe even smaller than that. It's okay to be scared, but you do know your mom and I will keep you safe, right? I promise."

She tweaked my ponytail, but it did nothing to cheer me up. I knew all about chances and statistics. Like: The chances of Angus Pfeffer's Tiger Moth model airplane's ending up on our roof had been a million to one—maybe more, since he'd launched it in Towne Park, on the other side of town. But that plane was still up there somewhere, getting all crumbly in the bright spring sunlight.

CHAPTER 13

Nickel had gone to the movies on Sunday afternoon without me. I was okay with that, since we had spent all morning analyzing the note and failing to come up with a plan to get to the lagoon.

By the time we finished lunch on Monday, he had told me the entire movie plot and given me a blow-by-blow description of every scene.

"If we practiced, we could adapt some of the acrobatic moves for Focus Pocus. The guy in *Dragon Claw* did this one where he ran up the side of a building and *bam!*" Nickel slapped his hand down on his cafeteria lunch tray. I jumped at least two inches out of my chair, whacking my knees on the underside of the table.

"He did a somersault straight off the wall." Nickel took a deep breath and rested back in his chair. "I'm pretty sure we could do that."

That wasn't the first time Nickel had lost his mind, so

I knew how to handle him. "One of us will break an arm if we try."

His mouth puckered. "Scratch that. I'm sure *I* could do it. You could pretend to be interested, you know."

"How many times have you broken your arm, Nickel Bugden?"

"Four. Five if you count the wrist fracture," he said, shrugging, as if he hadn't cried like a baby every single time.

"And how many times have I broken mine?" I asked.

"None. But that's because I'm more willing to sacrifice my body for the sake of improving Focus Pocus." He lifted one eyebrow. I think it was supposed to make him look confident, but he kind of looked like he was asking a question.

I sighed. "Or because you keep doing things even when I say you're going to get hurt."

Nickel squinted. "Maybe I can make decisions for myself. Maybe I don't need you to tell me what to do."

"Five broken arms says you do need to be told." I closed my lunch box and slipped it into my backpack. The slower and calmer I moved, the redder Nickel's ears got.

"Four broken arms and one wrist fracture, and one of the arms was from riding my bike, and you didn't even tell me not to do that."

I pushed back the sleeves of my sweater and held out my arms in front of me like a surgeon. "No broken arms.

I win. Now can I talk? Because I have something actually important to say."

Growling through white lips, Nickel said, "*Actually* important? We talked about your dad all day yesterday. Why is it that only your stuff matters and mine is wasting time?"

"Because we still haven't found a way to get to the Densdale Lagoon next weekend."

"We will. We always do." Nickel tapped his fingers on his food tray, hard enough to make his knife rattle on his plate. "I get that it's a big deal, but all we ever talk about anymore is your pretend father."

The word "pretend" stung like a wasp. I Doom Glared at him hard enough that he wriggled around in his chair like my eyeballs could shoot spikes at him.

" 'Pretend father'? He's not pretend. He's real and the most important thing ever. Much more important than some stupid movie."

Nickel folded his arms over his chest and scowled. "More important than Focus Pocus?"

"Much."

He jerked back like my words were a slap. I wanted to take them back, sort of, but words stuck around once you said them.

"Well, maybe he's a waste of time. Maybe . . . I don't know. Maybe he's not even worth finding, since he's the one that left you."

I swallowed hard, trying to get past a lump in my throat. When my voice finally came back, it sounded a bit strangled. "Because of a whole bunch of maybes, I can only talk about some ridiculous superhero club you made up when we were five?"

"Ridiculous? You don't think it's ridiculous when you need me to do stuff for you."

I didn't answer, even though I knew I should. The trouble with not speaking was that sometimes it was worse than saying something stupid.

Nickel's ears turned redder than his hair. Shoving his chair backward so hard it nearly fell over, he snatched up his tray and stalked off. And because I was more worried that he might be right about me using him than I was worried that I might lose my best friend and future husband, I didn't follow him.

• • •

Every kid should have their own superpower/mind-control club. In the beginning, Focus Pocus was known as the Nickels and Robyns Only Club, or N.A.R.O. We even made badges on a little machine I got for Christmas that year. Except people kept asking what the letters stood for, and this one girl called Robin tried to force us to let her in.

Mrs. Bugden hired a magician for Nickel's birthday who called himself the Master of Hocus Pocus, and our club name came from there. Unfortunately, I'd broken my badge maker by then.

During breaks at school, we'd plan and train and come up with fantastical solutions to all our day-to-day problems. Like one day in third grade when I turned up for lunch with my face red from crying.

"Kimber McLean did what?" Nickel asked.

"She told everyone that my hair's a wig! They all believed it. People keep tugging on it to see if it comes off."

"A wig?"

"Yeah. Gia said I should have gotten a pretty wig if I wanted to wear one at all. I don't even want to! My hair's just fine the way it is. Well, maybe if it weren't so curly, but that's all. It's the worst thing that ever happened to anyone, ever." I rubbed the heel of my hand into my eye to keep it from letting any more tears out.

"Ever? Like even worse than the *Titanic*?"

We'd just learned about that in history, and though no one would drown because of a fake-hair rumor, it felt at least that bad to me.

I nodded.

Nickel whistled. "Anyone can have boring hair, but yours is different. It's way cooler. Forget about them. We'll just have to prove we're not to be messed with. Watch this. Dime taught me a cool trick." He glanced around and settled on Gia Martelli's group of friends nearby. "Never fails."

He began to stare at the back of Gia's ponytailed head.

"Her hair's not gonna fall out from being stared at," I said.

Nickel ignored me and kept right on staring and staring and staring. It didn't take long before I got bored and nibbled at my lunch in between leftover sniffles from all the tears. A sandwich or so later, things got interesting.

Gia scratched at the back of her neck.

I took a bite of my apple.

Gia reached up to adjust her ponytail, and her shoulders twitched.

Nickel stared, and I ate a cookie.

One of Gia's friends looked around a bit. Then Gia did too. Soon everyone in her group was trying to figure out what was going on. Eventually, every one of them looked right at Nickel—who stared straight back at them.

"Ew! Don't stare!" Gia yelled at him.

I nudged his arm. "Quit it!"

He turned to me with a wide grin. "See how I did that?"

"Creeped Gia out?"

"Exactly. But think about it. I did it with nothing but my own eyeballs. That's it. That's power, if you ask me. Now all we have to do is try that on Kimber. Pretty soon people will wonder what we're staring at. She'll have the wibblies so bad she won't bug you again. You'll see."

And I did see.

Word got around, and Kimber never even glanced at either of us ever again, in case it set us off staring.

Over time we perfected several other powerful glares, but that was our first superpower and mind-control technique. I knew that if I had Nickel, we could solve any problem together.

So long as I had Nickel.

• • •

Mom would never let me go to Densdale alone, and Nickel wasn't talking to me. That left me very few options. Either I raised enough money to hire a cab, or Mr. Bones and his rickshaw would be my only ride.

I pulled the ancient tin lunch box I used for my most important treasures out from under my bed. Some of my treasures had been in there for years. I couldn't remember what had made most of them treasures in the first place, but it seemed wrong to throw them out. I fished out a grand total of fourteen dollars between bits of paper and glittery birthday cards.

I'd never hired a cab in all my life, but even I knew that fourteen dollars wouldn't get me there, much less pay the entry into Densdale Lagoon. I would need at least thirty dollars, I figured. Mom would pay me my allowance on Thursday, but it was only ten dollars.

There was one surefire way to make the remaining six dollars in a week—the toys on the magnet roof—and there was only one way to get there: through Grandma's window. That couldn't be done while she was at home, and she wouldn't be out for long enough until her salsa dance class the next week, which would be way too late. I needed to get her out of the house.

For two whole days, I waited for a miracle. If nothing happened soon, I'd have to borrow Mom's wand or sprinkle myself with fairy dust. It probably wouldn't help, but at least I'd look adorable.

Lucky for me, an extra last-minute party booking meant Mom and Grandma had to go shop for groceries, and I got my chance.

Grandma's room had nothing fairylike in it. Not a single sparkle. The wallpaper was printed with faded roses that ran wild, and she had a quilt with lacy edges draped over her bed.

I stood for a while in the middle of the room, trying not to walk right back out again. Grandma always thought the best of me, and that made sneaking around her room feel like the worst thing of all. Part of me hoped Mom and Grandma would get home early and I'd have no choice but to give up.

But they didn't come home. In fact, the window sat open a little, waiting for me. And right in the middle of the sill stood something I never thought I'd see again: the big decorated mason jar from Mom's room. What was it doing in here?

My heart fluttered and my hands shook as I picked up the jar. Even from the outside I could see it was stuffed to the brim with lots of different, obviously precious, some-things. But I'd seen Mom's treasures plenty of times. Glittery cards I had made for her birthdays, Mother's Days, and Christmases, all kept in a little tin box just like mine. The only difference between our boxes was that in Mom's, I was the treasure.

The jar didn't look like it had anything to do with me.

I knelt beside it on the floor. Its cap was scuffed, and rust filled every dent and scratch in the tin. Drawings and cutouts from magazines, mostly fairies and flowers and rabbits, were glued to the outside of the jar. Whatever Mom kept in there, she had never shared it with me, and she probably wouldn't want to now.

I bit my lip and gripped the jar in both hands. The lid didn't catch at all when I twisted it off, as if it wanted me to see inside. "I'm sorry, Mom," I whispered. "I won't steal anything. I promise."

I laid the lid on the floor beside me and carefully lifted out one item at a time.

Tickets to the theater. Some notes. A couple of folded envelopes and a Valentine's Day card. I stared, afraid to open it. Mom had never had boyfriends. Not a single one in my entire life, and before then, only my nameless father.

I peeked inside the card. It felt soft and worn, like it had been handled lots of times. On one half, a rose was pressed, flat and brown, stuck down with a bit of tape so that it covered the corny poem. Someone had written on the other side in wide, jerky letters.

Dear M.
Love you more than ever.
Can't wait to meet our baby.
Yours forever, B

B?
B!
Benjamin O'Malley! It had to be. That meant he knew about me, and he loved my mother and wanted to meet me. At least, he had when he'd written that note. I stared at the writing. *Dad touched this valentine.* I lifted it to my nose and breathed in deep, but I couldn't smell anything except the moldy scent of the rose.

I closed the card, tucked it in its place inside the jar, and carefully layered the other treasures back around it. Everything I knew of my dad existed only inside that jar, but I couldn't look at anything else in it. I'd already done enough. Guilt made my stomach squirm as I screwed the lid back on and left the jar on the floor behind the curtains so it wouldn't fall out when I climbed through the window.

My father loved my mother? I guess it made sense. They had to have loved each other once. But why wouldn't she tell me anything? How could I be almost twelve years old and not even know his name?

I needed to get to Densdale and meet him so he had a chance to love me, and I would have a chance to love him too. To do that, I needed money, which meant getting out on the roof and collecting some toys.

That was not going to be easy.

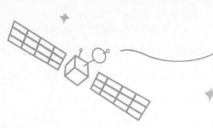

CHAPTER 14

I had already been in Grandma's room longer than I meant to. I couldn't waste any more time; I needed to get out the window and onto the roof. Mom and Grandma could be home at any minute, and I still had to collect as many toys as possible. Taking a deep breath, I sat on the sill and swung my legs outside.

The light glared off the lighter parts of the roof and made my eyes ache and blur, even though it wasn't a very bright day. The area right below the window was flat, but it was so close to the edge of the roof that one misstep would send me two floors down to the ground. If I kept close to the wall for a few feet, I'd be surrounded by the taller peaks of the roof and safe from falling. But I had to get that far first.

The roof creaked as my sneakers touched down. I kept myself from peeking at the sheer drop a few feet to my right, and focused on the colorful toys scattered around me.

Some of the Frisbees and kites must have flown a long way to get there, because there weren't enough kids in all our neighborhood to supply so many. Some were old and long forgotten, but some were brand-new and shiny. A few of the kites still had their tails in one piece.

Slow and careful, I moved across the roof, placing my feet on the nail holes to keep the strong beams underneath me. A few more feet and I'd be safe. In some places, the iron roofing had rusted and worn through until it looked like eyelet lace. Mrs. Cuthbert was right about the house being run-down. The roof was a rusted mess. It sure would not do much to stop a speeding satellite. Or a falling kid.

A bug took a sudden interest in my face, tickling my cheeks and trying to hide in my nostril. I pushed it away and sneezed it out, but it flew right back in. Doing my best to ignore it, I pushed on, slow and steady, until I reached the safe little valley between the roof mountains.

When I found a toy worth saving, I stuffed it into one of the plastic supermarket bags I carried in my pocket. Once a bag filled up, I tied it off and left it to be collected on the way back.

By the time I reached the edge of the safe, flat bit of roof, I had three bags full of moneymaking material. But it wasn't enough. The most I could raise out of all that was a few more dollars.

I pulled another bag from my pocket and stuffed in a toy plane with intact propellers, and a pair of golf balls

107

that had rolled down the slope into the mini gutter be-tween the two sections of roof. Calliope didn't even have a golf course.

I tried shinnying my way up the nearest bit of roof but slipped back down. Farther along, I gave it another try—carefully this time, because the rusted patches were the worst there. The rust scraped and stung my skin through my jeans, and my feet had no place to grip. I worked my way around the entire edge and struck out everywhere.

The almost-empty plastic bag dangled from my hand. My head throbbed from frustration and disappoint-ment. A person shouldn't have to try so hard just to get a parent.

I collected the bags and made my way out of the safe valley and back onto the last few flat feet to the window. My sneakers slipped on the flaky paint as I tossed the bags through the window. Clutching the sill, I hoisted myself up. It was a lot higher than it had seemed on my way out. I held on and walked my feet up the wall, but a board was frayed and the edge crumbled under my shoes.

Falling would be nothing compared to the world of trou-ble I'd be in if I had to call for help. I had to do this myself.

Looping my arm through the window, I kicked my leg up as high as I could. Puffing hard, I maneuvered myself inside—but my pant leg caught on the crumbly board on the way in.

I reached down and tugged at my jeans. They stuck

fast. So did my sleeve. When I tried to rip my arm loose, I almost fell out the window.

Grunting from the effort, I pulled my arm from inside my clothes and wriggled free of my sweater. On the third yank, a great tear opened up in my jeans, but my leg was un-snagged. At last, I dropped off the sill and onto the floor of my grandmother's bedroom.

"And what do you think you're up to, young lady?"

I flinched, and my pulse thudded hard in my temples. "Uh, collecting toys. For . . ." *Pant. Gasp.* "Charity?"

Grandma lifted her brows. "Oh, really? Let's donate them to charity, then."

Whether she believed me and wanted to help, or didn't and meant to call my bluff, I would lose my bags. Before I could make my mouth work, she had collected them all and was on her way out of the room.

"Grandma, wait." I jumped up from the floor and ran after her.

My foot caught on the torn piece of my pants. I stumbled and managed to stay upright, but then my toe snagged on a loose bit of carpet.

That floor was a lot harder than it looked.

• • •

Mom patted my shoulder from the backseat of Grandma's car. "It's not that bad. Six weeks and you'll be good as new. You can get all your friends to sign it."

I glanced down at the bright pink cast on my left arm. I only had one friend who mattered, and he wasn't talking to me. And if he had been, he'd have died from laughing after everything I'd said about him and broken arms. Not that I was capable of feeling embarrassment anymore. Having a flustered fairy for support in the ER had cured me forever. Despite her panic, Mom had taken the time to grab her wings and wand before we left the house.

"Just in case there's a sick child who needs cheering up," she'd said.

There was. Me. And the wings hadn't helped at all.

Grandma pulled her old Chevy to the side of the road behind Martyn's Drugstore. "One stop, then we'll get you home so your mother can spoil you."

Mom always made me chicken soup and garlic bread when I was sick or hurt, even if I couldn't eat them. She got fidgety and kept me where she could see me, sleeping on the blow-up mattress in my room if she had to. Grandma reckoned I got better faster just to get some time on my own, but that wasn't true. Okay, it was a little bit true. But mostly I liked it.

Grandma gave my leg a pat, hopped out of the car, and grabbed my bags from the backseat. As the toys disappeared into the huge yellow collection bin, I slumped back and groaned.

Mom leaned forward and wrapped her arms around my neck, her mouth right next to my ear. "Please don't ever, ever climb out on that roof again, okay? You might have gotten yourself killed. I couldn't bear that."

Technically, it was Grandma's tatty carpet that had been my undoing. Nothing had happened on the roof at all, except I'd torn a pair of perfectly good jeans and snagged a sweater. But I figured Mom wasn't in the mood for technicalities. It didn't matter much now, anyway.

Game over.

Goodbye, Densdale. Goodbye, usable arm. Goodbye, Dad.

Hello, satellite.

"I'm sorry, Mom."

I stared straight ahead, watching a cat strut across the parking lot like a general checking out the troops. My wrist throbbed in my lap, my fingers fat and useless.

As we pulled out to the street, a weird contraption wobbled past. It took me a minute to realize I was looking at a man and a bicycle-powered rickshaw half hidden beneath a long coat that flapped in the breeze as he pedaled.

"Old Mr. Bones," I whispered.

"Silly old fool. You'd think he'd be home by dinnertime," Grandma muttered, tapping her fingers on the steering wheel as she waited for him to pass.

"He's not an old fool," Mom said. "He gets the elderly to appointments for nothing and gives free rides to little kids at the fair. He's lovely."

Grandma sniffed. "Lovely old fool, then."

He didn't look lovely. He looked mad at the bike pedals and the world in general. The bike went pretty fast, though. Maybe fast enough to get to Densdale if we had a tailwind—and for only a dollar.

"How do people even hire him?" I asked.

"Usually see him parked outside Humphries's Gift and Guzzle on West Street. He sits out there all day waiting for Mack's Saloon to close," Grandma said.

West Street was an easy walk from our place.

I stared out the window all the way home, thinking, planning, and feeling just a little bit hopeful.

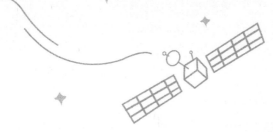

CHAPTER 15

It was almost dark when we got home from the hospital, but not too dark for us to see that a lot more than my arm had changed. Our whole front yard, for instance.

Grandma stood in the middle of our path, turning a slow circle with her mouth hanging open.

"My roses. What kind of criminal would do this to a person's roses?"

Instead of our wild and messy front yard, we had a mowed lawn with two perfectly weeded strips of garden and neatly trimmed rosebushes lining the path. I thought Grandma might cry. They had been ugly roses that grabbed your socks when you walked past, but they had been her ugly roses.

While Grandma groaned and stared, I spotted a slip of paper taped to our front door. Before she noticed it, I hurried up the step and pulled it down.

You're welcome.
AC

Mrs. Cuthbert.

Mom signaled me to hand her the note before Grandma saw it, and crumpled it into a ball in her fist. She held her finger to her lips and whispered, "Shhhh!"

Grandma marched around the back of the house, cursing and hollering for us to follow.

In the backyard, the gnarly old oaks and elms, as messy as ever, drooped and swayed in the breeze. The grass reached to my waist and caught my feet as I hurried to keep up.

Grandma petted the concrete birdbath, with its fuzzy moss. "At least it's still beautiful back here. This was Abigail Cuthbert's work, I'll bet you anything."

Trying to sound cheerful, I said, "It's not so bad. It's quite pretty out front."

"Pretty? Pretty! Where is the nature in that mess? My poor roses. She jailed them."

"They'll grow back fast. Don't worry," said Mom.

They certainly had seemed to stretch out over the path in a hurry last time.

"Not fast enough. They worked with the fairy theme. They—they looked woodsy and natural and beautiful."

"They're still pretty now. It's fine. Don't get all

stressed." Mom patted her shoulder, but that just made Grandma madder.

"I'm telling you. This is war."

It might be war, but I had my own battles. Grandma would have to fight that one on her own.

. . .

After dinner, Grandma clattered the dishes in the sink and stomped around the kitchen like she meant to squash an ant army. The news on TV didn't help.

"Invaded where now?" she muttered. "Have to blow things all out of proportion and cause a kerfuffle, don't they?"

I stopped scratching under my cast with one of her old knitting needles and stared laser beams at her. Feuding grandmas had no business judging other people.

She huffed and shrugged. "Course, if they went around calling people kleptomaniacs first, well, that'd be a different matter."

Someone knocked on the door, and Mom hurried off to answer it. Usually, she made me go, but being excused from regular duties was one benefit of having a broken arm.

On TV, the news anchor cleared her throat.

"Now for the latest on XR-26. Barry Cardogan, spokesman for NASA, has today explained the difficulty of predicting the outcome of the satellite's reentry. While predictions are expected to become more accurate as time goes on, there will be no way to estimate an exact landing time or zone. Here is Melissa Carpenter with more."

I held my breath as the camera switched to a pretty blond lady and a short, mostly bald man. "Mr. Cardogan, what does the lack of an accurate prediction mean for the public?"

The bald man nodded as the reporter spoke, and he took a deep breath as she finished. "Well, Melissa, XR-26's orbit is deteriorating in the way we expected, but I simply can't tell you with any precision where or when it might come down, although we may get better predictions closer to the time. It's important to remember that even if it were to come down in a populated area, the chances of it hitting anyone are tiny. No one has ever been hurt by space debris."

I clenched my good fist until my knuckles ached.

The worst, the very worst, thing about the satellite was that there was nothing to be done about it. NASA had no way to say for sure it wouldn't land near me. I couldn't negotiate with satellites, or outthink them, or outrun them. So I would concentrate on finding my dad, because I *could* do something about that.

Mom's voice echoed down the hallway, rising and falling in a friendly sort of way. A man answered her on the way back to the kitchen.

"So there's nothing we can do?" Mom sighed as Nickel's dad, Officer Bugden, followed her into the kitchen. Nickel would be tall like him one day, but hopefully Nickel would have more hair and slightly less tummy. Officer Bugden turned and saluted me. I grinned and waved back with my good arm.

"Evening, Shirley," he said, nodding at Grandma. "I'm sorry, ladies, but 'false imprisonment of roses' isn't a criminal act. Maybe we could call it trespassing, but what proof do you have it was even Abby Cuthbert?"

"This crime has her fingerprints all over it!" Grandma thumped the countertop with her fist.

Officer Bugden grinned. "Not literally, it doesn't. I'm sorry, Shirley."

Grandma sighed. "Can't argue with the law, now, can I?"

Nickel's dad leaned with his hand on the dining table. "You can, but it's probably best if you don't, all things considered. This isn't the first I've heard about this little feud between you two."

Grandma grinned and fiddled with a plate of fairy cupcakes.

"I had a very similar conversation with Mrs. Cuthbert a few days ago. Seems she had an unexpected shower and some sheets go missing off her line and turn up on your roof."

"They blew down the next day, good as new except for a bit of dirt," Grandma huffed, picking up the biggest cupcake and holding it out.

Officer Bugden grinned. "Lucky for you, I don't consider cupcakes to be a bribe." He took the cake and turned to me. "What's this I hear about you breaking your arm, little miss?"

I covered my cast with a cushion. "Don't tell Nickel."

He sucked in some air through his teeth. "Bad news, kiddo. He already heard from Jason Purcel, who heard it from Sarah Michaels, who heard it from Jenny Bristow, whose mom was in the ER with an attack of appendicitis today."

There had to be a law against parents passing on gossip, but if the cops couldn't even arrest rogue-gardener neighbors, it probably wouldn't help.

"I better mosey on. But do me a favor, ladies. Have a stern word with that roof of yours, will you? You see a lot in this job you'd rather never see again, but seeing Abby Cuthbert soaked to the skin and red as fury is beyond the call of duty." He tipped his hat and made for the door.

"Seems to me," Grandma said as she took her spot on the sofa beside me while Mom saw Mr. Bugden out, "that if the law doesn't care about trespassing and reckless gardening, Abigail Cuthbert better watch out."

The "law" hadn't left yet and yelled back from the porch, "I'm gonna go ahead and pretend I didn't hear that, Shirley!"

"Oops," said Grandma with a grin.

CHAPTER 16

Nickel didn't show up at school until after lunch the next day. All through our afternoon classes, I tried to say something, but my mouth wouldn't work. I peeked at him from behind my books and made drowning-fish faces without any sound coming out.

When it was the same on Friday, I knew I had to say something. The Densdale Lagoon get-together was only a day away, and even if I could take the rickshaw, it would all be so much easier with Nickel's help—and his allowance.

I made my move during afternoon recess.

Clutching a marker, I waited at Nickel's locker for him to pick up his backpack, the way he did every afternoon. "Hey," I said.

He didn't turn around. "Hi."

"I, um, wondered if you'd like to sign my cast."

For a whole minute—I counted every second—he

didn't move. I'm not sure he even breathed. "I thought you were too clever to break your arm," he said at last.

I held out the marker. "Please?"

He signed his name, capped the pen, and handed it back to me. "There." He pulled his backpack from his locker and closed the door.

When he turned to leave, I tugged at his sleeve with my good hand. "Wait. I wanted to apologize."

Nickel sighed. "I hoped you wouldn't."

Confused, I let his arm go. "You don't want to be my friend anymore?"

He stared at a spot on the floor as far away from me as possible. "I wanted you to make up with me sometime when you didn't need me to help you get to Densdale tomorrow."

I took a step back and swallowed, hard, because he was right. Horribly, disgustingly right.

No one had ever been a worse friend than me.

I watched his hunched-over back as he walked away.

• • •

The next morning, the wind ruffled the kitchen curtains while Mom dished out pancakes for breakfast. I hoped old Mr. Bones rode in any weather.

Mom put a plate in front of me. Already she was a flurry of sparkles and spangles, wings and wonder. "This is one for the record books. What got you out of bed this early?"

Before I went to sleep the night before, I had planned my story out. But now that the time had come to speak the lie, it stuck in my mouth. I was a terrible friend, and after that day I would be a terrible daughter as well.

I chewed my pancake slowly and swallowed it with a gulp. "I'm going to Nickel's house to try and make up with him."

Mom knew all about the non-Dad parts of our fight, and a smile spread across her face. "You're going to apologize?"

I nodded. "I was a jerk." That part was true.

"It takes a big person to admit it when they're wrong. Your little club's important to Nickel."

Had I made Focus Pocus sound as silly as that during our fight?

No. I'd done worse.

"I'm proud of you, Bob." Mom reached over from her side of the table and patted my hand. I wished she wouldn't. That one word, "proud," was almost enough to make me confess everything and never leave the house again. Except this might be my last chance to find my dad before the satellite hit.

The pancake in my tummy squirmed around. It obviously didn't like being in the stomach of a liar. "I better go," I said. I scraped my plate clean and put it in the dishwasher.

When I opened the front door, something strange hung above the steps, fluttering and twisting in the wind. It was a long string with dozens of ribbons tied to it. The string went up past the porch roof and the windows, and all the way to the gutter that ran between my bedroom and the bathroom.

On the end of the string was a diamond-shaped kite taller than me, maybe even taller than Mom. It sat at a jaunty angle, shuddering in the wind like the house wore it as a hat. The old rooster weather vane had skewered it right through the middle.

I glanced at Mrs. Cuthbert's house. No sign of her yet. I tugged at the kite, trying to get it down before she saw. Whatever the thing was made out of, it stuck fast. I pulled and yanked on the string until my good hand was covered in deep score marks. The kite stayed right where it was.

"Stupid house!" I screamed, kicking at the string and missing. "I hate you, you stupid, rotten house. What's the matter with you?"

I yanked one more time on the string—which did nothing—and stomped off. It was a lot easier to stomp now that the roses grew upright instead of all over the path.

"Are you going to find the owner of that thing?" Mrs.

Cuthbert asked from somewhere close by. "It's huge. Probably worth a lot of money."

I jumped and spun around to see her picking dead rose blooms from the bushes in her front yard. She still had her bathrobe and slippers on.

"Yes. Later," I said.

"Later? Someone might have reported it missing. Someone might call the police."

Heat burst into my cheeks. I knew who that "someone" would be. My mouth filled up with all the anger I had tried to keep in since the last time she had let me have it. "Well, go right ahead, you horrible old busybody."

Mrs. Cuthbert's mouth dropped open. "I beg your pardon, you rude little madam? Everything I've done has been for the good of this community and, whether you like it or not, for the good of your family as well."

"No, it hasn't. You called the police and ruined Grandma's yard. You pretend you work for the FBI and mind everybody else's business." A horrible shooting pain in my sore arm forced me to unclench my fists. I gritted my teeth instead. "And we're not klepto—kep—thieves either."

The old woman's face turned red enough for steam to come out of her ears. She threw a handful of dead roses onto the ground and pointed at me. "Oh, pretending, am I? What about your mother, hmm? Flouncing around here dressed like a fairy, even when she's off duty. And what about your grandmother, poking her nose into my business all the time? She's the real busybody."

Not wanting Grandma or Mom to hear and come out to make things worse, I lowered my voice. "My mom is being herself, and there's nothing wrong with that. Grandma isn't the one peeking through our fence with binoculars."

"There's plenty round here who agree with me!" She waved her hand like there was a fly she wanted to swat away. "Some people round here might feel sorry for that mother of yours, but not me. I know better." She headed inside.

"What? Why would anyone feel sorry for Mom?" I called after her, but she'd already gone.

Because of Dad? Did people feel sorry because he left us?

I stood there for a while, the wind tossing bits of leaves and dirt against my bare legs. Mrs. Cuthbert wanted to cause trouble. She wanted me to run to Grandma and make her mad.

Tears dribbled down my cheeks before the wind could dry them. I blinked back the rest, stuck out my chin, and walked off toward Humphries's Gift and Guzzle on West Street. No one would need to feel sorry for us again. Not after today.

CHAPTER 17

Even though I knew Mrs. Humphries, I'd never been inside her store before. When Mom shopped at the Gift and Guzzle, she made me wait in the car so I wouldn't beg for candy. I crossed the fingers on my good hand for luck. I shook bad thoughts out of my head and looked around for a sign of old Mr. Bones.

The Gift and Guzzle used to be a gas station when Mom was my age. The old tin Texaco sign took up most of one side wall, along with newer ones advertising cola and Barney's Bait Shop. The roof of the porch that ran along the front drooped at one end and shuddered in the wind like a twitchy eyebrow. A few wooden barrels, filled with small shrubs and sprinkled with cigarette butts, were lined up on either side of the door.

There was no sign of Mr. Bones or his rickshaw.

A little bell above the shop door tinkled as I peeked inside. Mrs. Humphries had her back to me, humming to herself while she tidied the rows of leather belts, cowboy hats, and grizzly bear candles. She turned with a smile at the sound of the bell.

"Well now, if it isn't Robyn Goodfellow. I was sorry to hear about your arm."

News got around Calliope faster than Mr. Bones could ever pedal. "Uh, thanks. It's not that bad," I said. "Is it true Mr. Bones waits around here sometimes?"

Mrs. Humphries lifted her eyebrows and put down the bottle opener she had been dusting. "Mr. Bones? Oh, yes. Every day. All day. He'd be my best customer if he bought more than a can of soda per day. I've had raccoon families move in under the store that were easier to get rid of than him." Smiling, she shook her head. "And don't you go mentioning the raccoons to anyone, or I'll deny it cold, you hear me?"

Raccoons living under your store sounded like a good-luck charm to me, but I could see how some people in Calliope might overreact. "I hear you. Has Mr. Bones been around today?"

"He was out there a few minutes ago. Some fool probably hired that contraption of his. They'll learn that lesson in a hurry."

"What lesson? What will he do?" My eyes got so wide they dried out a bit.

Mrs. Humphries chuckled. "Don't look so startled.

He's harmless. Just a bit . . . shall we say . . . stern? That rickshaw, though. Rattles your bones. Ha, I guess that's where the nickname came from."

I swallowed nervously past a lump in my throat. "Okay. Thank you."

I almost had the door closed again before she stopped me. "What on earth do you want with Jack Bones?"

I was about to tell her the truth when the perfect answer popped into my head. "School project. We're studying transport, and I, uh, thought the rickshaw was interesting."

Mrs. Humphries rocked back on her heels. "Interesting? That would be one way to describe it. So long as you're not planning to ride in it. Your mom would be devastated if she lost you too."

"Lost me too?" Like she lost my dad?

Her face turned that strange shade of pale adults always had when they realized they had talked themselves into a situation and had no idea how to get out.

"Oh, look there," Mrs. Humphries said, her smile too wide and plastic. She pointed out the door as Mr. Bones's coat fluttered past. I knew she wouldn't tell me any more than anyone else would. So I gave Mrs. Humphries a quick wave and hurried after Mr. Bones.

At the edge of the porch, I watched as he maneuvered the rickshaw against the wall, out of the wind. Every joint in his body popped and cracked as he eased his hunched self off the bike seat.

"Hello," I said in a small voice.

He turned slowly to face me. That close, I could see why everyone called him Mr. Bones. All that showed under the hood of his coat were dark eye sockets, pointy cheekbones, and a sucked-in mouth. The skin covering it looked dry and tight, like he might be nothing but a skeleton after all.

"Yesss?" he asked, drawing out the s into a lizard's yawn.

My mouth opened and my tongue moved, but nothing came out.

He gave up on me and turned back to his bike. It looked about as bony as he did. So did the rickshaw. It was nothing but a pair of painted planks with wheels and a beat-up canopy overhead.

He bent over to pinch his tires, ignoring me.

This was stupid. If he was scary or . . . whatever, people would not keep hiring him to drive them around. Mrs. Humphries had called him stern, but if I could survive Mrs. Cuthbert, I could survive a cranky rickshaw driver.

I needed to suck it up and speak. "I—um—can I hire you?"

He stood up straight and spun around with a wide smile on his face. At least, I think it was a smile. It looked more like a dark gap in his face. No teeth.

"Why didn't you say so? My price is a dollar. No haggling. You pay your dollar, fair and square." He sounded different now, lispy and almost friendly.

"No, sir. A dollar is fine."

"Climb aboard, kid."

Sitting on that hard seat was like waiting outside the dentist's office: I had no idea what might happen, but I knew it would be uncomfortable. The old man eased himself onto his seat and leaned around to face me. He held out a hand as white and bony as his face. "Dollar."

I dropped the bill into his hand and wriggled backward in my seat.

"Where to?" he asked.

"Um, the Densdale Lagoon, please."

He froze with my money halfway to his pocket. "You what now?"

"The—the Densdale Lagoon. It's a water park. In Densdale. Like a lagoon."

What an idiot I was. This guy was old. The bike looked even older. I never saw him anywhere outside Calliope. He probably couldn't come close to making it that far.

"Densdale? What in the name of all things Calliope do you want to go there for? The swimming hole not good enough for you?" He snorted so hard that steam should have come out of his nostrils. "Not a thing you can do there that you can't do here."

Of course he wouldn't go to Densdale. This was a stupid idea.

"I'm sorry." I moved to jump out of the rickshaw, but he held out that awful hand to stop me.

"You paid your dollar, you take your ride," he said.

• • •

The rickshaw had looked fast the day I broke my arm, but it felt faster once I was on board. I squinted and held on tight with my good hand. Mr. Bones's coat snapped around like a superhero's cape, slapping my legs if I relaxed them.

"You must be fit," I said, trying to make conversation with the hunched-over man in front of me.

No answer.

"Because, you know, all that pedaling."

Still no answer.

Biting my lip to keep myself from talking any more, I concentrated on not becoming roadkill.

"The wilds of Densdale right ahead," Mr. Bones said as we passed the sign on the town border. It read YOU'RE LEAVING CALLIOPE. AIN'T TOO LATE TO CHANGE YOUR MIND!

There was no sign welcoming us to Densdale, because Densdale thought we'd been a part of the city all along. If you looked at a map, you'd agree with them too. You had to be from Calliope to know better.

The tree belt on the edge of town could have been a portal to a whole other universe. On one side, we were a bicycle-powered rickshaw on an almost empty road. On the other side, we were a very small, very flimsy contraption among a million cars whose drivers knew lots of curse words.

Between the beeps and revving engines, I heard Mr. Bones mutter something rude about Densdale. He snarled, leaned over his handlebars, and pedaled like a bear was on our tail.

Getting to Densdale was the easy part; you only had to leave Calliope to manage that, and Calliope was pretty small. Densdale was not. An hour of frantic pedaling later and we were less than a third of the way to the lagoon.

This plan was the worst.

We sped around corners, the rickshaw tilting until there was nothing but air under one tire, sometimes both. Bugs and the wind whizzed past my ears. Mr. Bones had a pretty relaxed policy on stop signs too.

We zipped through sets of traffic lights, tires screeching all around us. Mr. Bones cackled like a witch from a bad fairy tale. "Ha!" he yelled, swerving around a pedestrian in a crosswalk.

My heart pounded until I could barely hear the traffic. If I survived the trip, it would be a bigger miracle than if the satellite missed my house.

We finally slowed down around the halfway mark. Overhead, the clouds grouped together like they had a party planned, and we had to travel straight into the wind. The old man shoved his coat hood back off his head. Underneath, his scalp was as white and shiny as a polished skull. I shuddered and checked whether Alyssa's note was still inside my cast, where I'd tucked it that morning. Having it there felt like safety, like I'd find out about my dad for real, that day.

Mr. Bones pulled the rickshaw into a small side street and stopped. He twisted around in his seat to face me, and little dribbles of sweat slid over his pointy cheekbones. "You got your heart set on this whole lagoon thing?"

My muscles were exhausted from holding on. They gave up when he said that, and I slumped back in the rickshaw. There was no way one old man could get us to the lagoon on time.

He let out a sigh that sounded exactly like the wind whistling under the roof at home. "Let me catch my breath, then we'll carry on."

A little bit of hope tickled inside me, but it went out again. "No. This was a dopey idea. I'm sorry."

Muttering something about "sad eyes" and "sucker," Mr. Bones got back on the bicycle. "This had better be about something more important than swimming, or I swear . . ."

"It is," I promised.

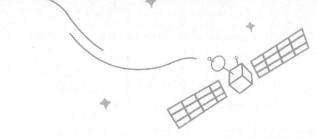

CHAPTER 18

M r. Bones, his rickshaw, and I were on the road to the Densdale Lagoon for three hours in total. During that time, I learned how to drive a rickshaw one-handed and took a turn pedaling whenever we came across a quiet side road. While Mr. Bones rested, he told strange, pointless stories.

"Once, I drove Mayor Tippins almost this far," he said during my last turn pedaling. "I worked hard that day. He ain't a small man."

"Mayor Tippins? Cool." It was not really cool. Mayor Tippins wasn't a real mayor any more than Calliope was a real town. But his great-granddaddy had been mayor before Densdale ate Calliope, and everyone acted like he had the job now. Including him.

"Yup."

"And then what?" I asked, panting as I stood up on the pedals to get the rickshaw up a slight rise.

"I drove him home again." Yep. Weird stories with no point.

"How come you decided to give everyone rickshaw rides?" I asked, slowing down from tiredness.

"Obvious, isn't it? If it weren't for me, people might start wanting a bus route through town, and then what, eh? Next thing we know, Densdale's getting all smug and thinking it owns us. I do it for the town." He chuckled to himself. "Besides, a couple of the old ladies I drive around bake me cakes and cookies."

I laughed and pulled over for him to take his turn.

By the time we had the lagoon in sight, I didn't think he was scary at all, or even that cranky. Frightening looks did not mean frightening man—at least, not in this case. He pulled the rickshaw into the almost-empty lagoon parking lot and let out a huge sigh of relief. "We did it."

"We did!" I clambered out of the rickshaw and looked around. "There aren't many cars."

"Don't worry about that. It's the weather. There's still plenty of afternoon left."

I smiled harder than I had since the satellite news broke. Because Mr. Bones was as close to a friend as I had left, I held out my cast for him to sign and handed him my marker.

"First time I ever signed one of these things." He grinned toothlessly and scrawled *Jack Bones* in raggedy letters across the middle of my cast, then added a skull and crossbones as a sort of signature.

"Thanks," I said, peering up at the sky. There were a lot of clouds hanging around, the thick purple-gray sort that held nothing but trouble. Sunshine was an important part of any trip to the Densdale Lagoon. The pools were not heated, and the whole thing was outdoors.

"I could bring you back next weekend, when the weather is better," Mr. Bones said, and I could tell he hoped I would say yes. I promised myself I would take regular rickshaw rides if I survived the satellite. "Your sainted momma wouldn't be happy with me if I left you here in the rain."

"You know Mom?" I asked.

"Who in Calliope doesn't? Lovely girl. Lovely. Shame about, you know, everything."

"Everything?" I didn't know, but by then I had a pretty good idea. My dad. I couldn't bring myself to ask. Not that day. Not when the truth about Benjamin O'Malley was so close I almost tasted it. "It's okay. I'm meeting some friends here. It kind of has to be today," I said.

"Then you get on in there and have some fun," he said. "If you need a ride home, I can take you back. Have to get there myself, after all."

I hugged him. Just like that. I threw my good arm around his neck and hugged him. "Thank you, but I'll have a ride by then." At least, I hoped I would.

Chuckling to himself again, he hopped back onto the bicycle seat. "I'll stop by and check before I head home, just in case."

He waved and pedaled off. When all I could see of the rickshaw was the *Toot and I'll Pedal Slower* bumper sticker, I turned and headed for the huge iron gates that led into the park.

There were only a few cars in the lot. They had to belong to my new family. Maybe they had carpooled or were running late. A thought niggled at my nerves. What if the get-together had been canceled because of the weather, or they had all gone home before I even arrived?

Before I could worry too much, a car pulled into the lot behind me.

A police cruiser. Nickel's dad's cruiser, in fact.

Adrenaline made a dash through my veins, although I wasn't sure if it was from fear or excitement. I stood there in the middle of the lagoon parking lot with dust and used tickets blowing into my hair, staring as my former best friend and future husband climbed out of his dad's car. He had on a pair of baggy swim shorts with an even baggier T-shirt, and his towel was draped around his neck.

"I'll be back at five," his dad said, waving as he reversed the car to drive away.

One moment I was numb with shock, and the next . . . I screamed.

Because sometimes your best friend turns up when you need him the very most, and the only thing that makes sense is to holler at the top of your lungs.

Nickel froze. He said something, but I couldn't hear over my own noise.

I ran at him and threw my arms around his neck, clocking him on the back of the head with my cast as I did. I had hugged more males in the past ten minutes than in the whole rest of my life. "You're here!"

He let me hug him for a bit before he pulled away. "Okay. Enough. Whatever."

I stepped back, grinning. "Thank you. And I truly am sorry."

Nickel shrugged, but his mouth looked tight, like he wanted to keep a smile from slipping out. "Me too. I wasn't very nice about your dad. Would have been here sooner, but I thought you were hitchhiking. We drove around looking for you."

"You're here—that's what matters."

"Yeah, you might not think so when I tell you the rest." He grimaced. "Your grandma kind of knows you're not at my house like you said you were."

I stopped breathing and froze.

"Don't panic. She doesn't know about your dad. We stopped by to pick you up, but you were already gone. Your grandma said you were headed to our place, so Dad told her we'd find you and he'd bring you home tonight.

Dad thinks I told you I'd be here this weekend, and that you probably came here to find me."

I breathed a little bit. "Will he tell Mom and Grandma that I'm here?"

He shrugged. "Probably. You know parents."

When Mom found out I'd come all the way to Densdale on my own, I would not be leaving my room for the rest of my life. There would be no more chances to find Benjamin O'Malley. Today was all I had.

I nudged Nickel's shoulder and pointed toward the entrance gate. "We should get inside. Come on."

"I don't like the look of this. Shouldn't there be more cars?" he asked.

I counted the cars I could see. "Two sedans and a station wagon. That's enough to transport at least some of my family."

The closer we got to the gate, the less likely it seemed that those cars belonged to anyone but maintenance workers. Only the wind made any noise. There was no splashing. No happy squeals. "Are you thinking what I'm thinking?" I asked.

"I dunno. What are you thinking?"

A big shiver rumbled through me. "Zombie apocalypse."

Nickel laughed. "I am so not thinking what you're thinking."

"I can call your dad now," the guard said. He sure was a lot more help than the guard who had kept everyone trapped in the theater.

A little ray of hope shone inside me. "Nickel, I could use the money I saved for the entrance fee to hire a cab and ride to the *What's Current* offices. The reporter talked to my family in the news story. She might have a phone number or address."

Nickel screwed up his nose. "They'll be closed on a Saturday."

That stupid little ray of hope fizzled out. "Oh." I gave the security guard a miserable smile. "I guess you better call his dad. Thank you," I said.

The guard took Officer Bugden's number and walked away. I slid down the gate to sit on the hard concrete.

Nickel sat beside me. "I'm sorry."

"I hoped, that's all." That horrible prickling started up in my nostrils until I had to stare very hard at a pebble on the ground to make the feeling go away. "No swimming. No lagoon. No brothers and sisters. And no—" I stopped before saying "dad," because just thinking it made the prickling worse.

"You couldn't swim anyway with a cast."

I looked down at it. "I was only going to wade at the edges, not get wet. I was here to find Dad."

"He's probably a jerky turkey anyway," Nickel said, nudging me with his elbow.

By the time we reached the entrance, we bot[h]
thinking exactly the same thing.

The wrought-iron gates were locked shut. H[anging]
from the padlocked chain was a big sign that read [CLOSED]
DUE TO BAD WEATHER.

I took the bars in my hands and pressed my face a[gainst]
them, trying to see inside. Fake palm trees swished
and forth like on a hurricane news report. The surfa[ce of]
the water in the pools rippled and rolled. I'd only w[orried]
about whether Mr. Bones would be open for busine[ss, not]
whether the lagoon would be.

"I hate everything," I said, letting the bars pre[ss the]
frames of my glasses into my cheeks and stripe me [like a]
pink-and-white zebra.

"Sorry, kids. Park's closed," said someone with a [tired]
but cheerful voice from somewhere nearby. I jumped
and saw a man walking toward us on the other si[de of]
the bars. He wore a security guard's uniform and [car]
ried a gigantic flashlight, even though it wasn't dark[, just]
gloomy.

"Yeah, we read the sign," said Nickel.

"You got a ride home?" the guard asked.

Nickel looked at me. "Dad's coming for us later[," he]
said.

Someday maybe I could say the same words. Not [to]
day, though. Again.

"I wouldn't care if he was," I said. Although I probably would.

"I bet he steals the TV remote and never lets you watch cartoons. Probably picks his teeth with his pinky nail." Nickel pretended to gag and choked out a laugh. "Like Uncle Mal."

Nickel always could make me giggle, even when I didn't want to. All I had to do was think about the barbecue at Nickel's house the past summer, when his uncle Mal had turned up in an unbuttoned Hawaiian shirt, with greasy hair and a soggy-looking baseball cap. He made Mr. Bones look downright adorable. If I imagined my father like that, it made things a bit easier.

A satellite was still on its way to squash my house, probably with me in it. People would laugh when they read the story in the newspaper, because of my stupid, embarrassing name. I had no father to help me change it or to remember me. In fact, I had no father at all. I did have Nickel back, though, and that mattered almost as much.

Fat drops of rain splashed onto the concrete around us. Nickel pulled his towel over his head, and I got mine from my bag and did the same.

"Mrs. Cuthbert and Mrs. Humphries and Mr. Bones all know about my father. I just know it. But they won't say anything," I said.

"Not their story to tell, I guess," Nickel said, and it was irritatingly true.

"It is my story, though. I just don't know it."

Nickel shrugged. "Whatever. I'm just saying. Your mom seems kinda . . . breakable. Maybe they don't want to upset her. She might lose it and cover the whole town in glitter."

"My mom's as tough as anyone else's mother," I muttered. No one in Calliope was normal. Mom was a bit less normal than most, maybe. I didn't think she could change. I didn't think I wanted her to.

The rain beat down harder every second, which was a good thing. It washed away the heat in my cheeks, and even *I* couldn't tell whether any tears sneaked out of my eyeballs.

We heard a car, wipers beating furiously, driving across the parking lot toward us before we could see it through the rain. "Dad was fast getting back," said Nickel.

The car drove straight up to the gate and stopped. It was an ordinary station wagon, not a police cruiser. The driver's window rolled down, and inside I saw the mom I had met at the theater. The same one who had given me the note. Alyssa.

"I thought you might be here," she said.

CHAPTER 19

Alyssa climbed out of the car into the miserable rain of the Densdale Lagoon parking lot. Smiling, she opened the hatch door of her station wagon so we could sit under it, out of the rain. It mostly helped.

"We had to change the meet-up to next week because the park closed. I had no idea how to get hold of you." She gestured at the boy hunched over his phone in the back-seat. "This is my son, Mikey."

I closed my eyes and hoped it would be a different Michael, but when I opened them, the first thing I saw was him. White hair. White eyelashes. Big jerk. Michael didn't even peel his nose away from his phone or say hello when his mom mentioned him. By the sound of the beeps and explosions, I guessed he was playing some army game.

"Not Mikey. Michael! How many times?" He shouted it loud enough that we all jumped a little.

"Tell me more about your story," Alyssa said, ignoring her kid. "Why don't you ask your mom about your dad?"

Michael lifted his knuckles to his eyes and screwed them around like he was rubbing at fake tears. "Wah, wah. I want my daddy." He reminded me more of Dameon Swenson than of someone I could be related to.

If I told Alyssa that Mom never spoke about Dad, she probably wouldn't tell me anything either. Moms always stuck together.

"I—I only found out about him recently," I lied. Again. And again. "I haven't had a chance to ask her since."

Alyssa frowned. I hoped that meant she disapproved of unhelpful mothers and not my terrible acting.

"Her mom is away for work right now," Nickel said. He thought on his feet way better than I did.

"I need to know. For my peace of mind and all that," I said. It came out sounding a lot more sincere than it probably should have. At least it made Alyssa look thoughtful as she rummaged around in the junk behind the backseat.

She found a frayed old towel and handed it to us to dry off some of the rain, since our towels were even wetter than we were. "What's the hurry?"

"The satellite." I blurted it right out.

She laughed. "Satellite? You're not panicking about that, are you?"

That was it. My words dried up. I shot Nickel a desperate look.

"She has good reason," he said. "Long story. But if you have time, maybe you could take us to meet Benjamin O'Malley? We're free right now, since my dad won't be here for a while."

Go see him now? My heart jumped into my throat and half strangled me. Was I ready? My hair needed drying and some emergency treatment to fix the weird clumpy thing it was doing from being rained on. But it wasn't like I had another chance.

"That would be great!" I said.

Alyssa stared straight ahead. "No, no, no. Slow down a bit. Ben, he—well, he's just my best guess if your dad is a member of our family. He hasn't been the same since he went to Iraq. How old are you?"

"I'm almost twelve."

She made a humming sound. "I guess—that could add up about right. Ben had a girlfriend before he left, but they broke up. We never met her. Wow, this would just be so bizarre. But I'll need to talk to him first. He wouldn't cope well with something like this being sprung on him. I mean, who would?"

I crossed my arms to hold myself together and keep from panicking. "You don't understand. This is my only chance."

She waved a hand at me. "Trust me. He's not going anywhere. He barely leaves the house."

Nickel opened his mouth and shut it again, turning to

look at me. I gestured to encourage him to keep talking. "Robyn can't get back to Densdale. People in Calliope don't like coming here."

Alyssa laughed. "So I heard. What's with that? They *are* here!"

Outside Calliope, it did sound pretty weird.

"We know," Nickel and I said at once.

Alyssa said, "Look, kids, I'm sorry. I can't just drive you away without your mom's permission, much less introduce you to a man who might be your father. I'd be furious if someone did that to me and my kid." Michael cursed loudly from the backseat, and Alyssa groaned. "Unless they promised not to bring him back, anyway. Look, talk to her this week, and if she agrees, have her call me. Then, if Ben is okay with it, I'll pick you up next weekend."

That was a great offer, but Mom would never give me permission. Not in a million weekends. Alyssa didn't say anything else except to ask for my phone number. I pretended we didn't have one and gave her my email instead.

I almost blurted out the truth. About Mom's sneakiness when it came to Dad. About how I needed to change my name and have someone take me for ice cream and buy me an iguana, and about a million other things that couldn't wait for even another week. But what then? She still wouldn't help without talking to Mom, and all my secrets would be out.

Luckily, Officer Bugden's car rolled into the lot, windshield wipers thumping.

"That's my dad," Nickel said.

Alyssa looked a bit sorry when she smiled at me. "Don't worry. We'll talk again next weekend. I promise. It's only a week."

Nodding, I stood up and wrapped my arms around myself. How could a day that had started with a rickshaw ride, full of hope, have gone so wrong?

"Mikey, say goodbye, at least," Alyssa said.

He glanced over his shoulder. "Goodbye, at least," he said, and went right back to his game.

That did it. Family was overrated. I could definitely do without them. Or most of them. Not that I had a choice.

"Thanks for everything." I straightened out my clothes and waved.

. . .

It took all my Focus Pocus breath training to get through the drive home without crying. The last thing I needed was for Officer Bugden to escort me inside. I'd have enough explaining to do as it was.

"You be home by eight, son," Officer Bugden said as he pulled up outside my house.

"Yessir."

"You're coming too?" I whispered as we got out of the car.

"Of course," he said.

Before he could change his mind, I dragged him inside after me and slammed the door. Almost right away, someone knocked on the other side.

"Dad?" Nickel whispered as we stared at the closed front door.

Another knock. A bit louder this time. I pressed my hands against the wood, hoping it would absorb some of the noise. Then I peeked through the peephole.

A woman with brown hair. "It's Alyssa," I hissed. Had she followed us home just so she could blab to Mom?

"She knows we're in here. Maybe we should let her in?" Nickel whispered.

Desperately, I looked from the door to him and back. "Mom will find out about Benjamin O'Malley. I'll be done for."

Shrugging, Nickel joined me in pushing on the door.

Mom hurried down the hall from the party bathroom, dragging a small girl in a tutu by the hand. "What on earth are you doing? Who's there?"

I spun around and pressed my back to the door. "It's a wrong number."

"And I'm the one that people around here call eccentric." Mom rolled her eyes and jerked her thumb in the air. "Hop it."

Nickel got out of the way, but I stayed there with fists and teeth clenched. "I can't. It's a . . . political protest."

My extra couple of inches since the new year meant she could not lift me off my feet anymore. She knew plenty of other tricks, though—the sort that involved tickles and vicious goosing. In a few seconds, she had the door open.

But I was wrong.

It wasn't Alyssa. A family-sized station wagon was parked in our driveway outside, and a woman stood at the door with her arms folded and a great big frown line between her eyes.

"Nice of you to answer," she said.

"I'm sorry. My daughter has lost her tiny mind," Mom said, handing the small girl over to her mom.

"I'm very sorry," I said.

"We thought you were a vacuum cleaner salesperson," Nickel said.

Mom scowled at us. "From now on, I will be in charge of opening the door."

I sighed with relief.

From then on, it wouldn't matter. Unless Alyssa showed up again.

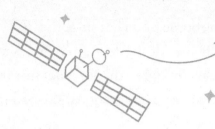

CHAPTER 20

Nickel was at my house. On purpose.

The last time that happened, he went home with two small handprints in green frosting on the back of his brother's real leather jacket. It would not have been so bad, except his brother had warned him he would string him up by his shorts if he ever touched that jacket. It earned Nickel a near-fatal wedgie, and he had not visited since.

That was probably why his face was screwed up like he was in terrible pain.

"They're only little kids," I said.

Another couple of toddlers appeared at the Fairy Wonderland door. Mom frantically moved them into a group like a herd of sticky, colorful sheep. "Time to get into your own clothes before your parents get here, my dears," she said.

She started on one child, but another sneaked down the hall and picked up the telephone. Mom had to leave the others to keep her from calling Timbuktu. Every time Mom grabbed one kid, another made a run for it. There were only five or six kids, but they seemed to multiply. Mom's cheeks were hot pink, and she looked ready to explode.

"That does it! Bob, Nickel, grab a kid and dress it."

"I am not an it!" said the small girl she had by the collar.

"Of course you aren't, sweetie," Mom said through clenched teeth.

I reached out and grabbed a toddler with bulging eyes as he streaked by in a pixie costume, waving his arms and hollering something about baseballs. "It wouldn't hurt to consider natural food colorings, you know, Ma."

She rolled her eyes at me, but I could tell a small part of her agreed.

Nickel backed slowly toward the door. "I—I think I'll wait on the porch," he said, reaching behind for the doorknob.

"Do not move, young man. The fairy room—go clean it before the parents arrive!" Mom waved him away.

"W-what if one of the kids touches me?"

She gave him a scathing look. "They are children, Nickel, not bacteria."

Personally, I thought they were a bit of both.

Looking a little dejected and a lot terrified, Nickel shuffled off. His bedroom at its tidiest still looked worse than the Fairy Wonderland after a day of parties, so I didn't hold out much hope for the state of the room when he was done with it.

"Hold still," I told the small toddler squirming in my hands.

The little kid looked up at me with what I thought were huge brown eyes. Turned out they were actually blue with superwide pupils. It was a symptom of sugar psychosis, I was pretty sure.

He panted. "I gonna splode."

"How about you explode after you have your own clothes on?" I said.

He screwed up his face, clenched his fists, and made a noise like a steaming kettle. After a few seconds, his eyes opened again. "I di'n't splode."

"Sorry," I said. "Maybe next time."

Deflated, the boy pointed out his own pile of clothes on the shelf in the hallway. Aside from a few mismatched buttons, I got him dressed and moved on to the next one. I had to stop in the middle when the next parents arrived.

Two doorbells later and we were on the last of the kids.

Mom, Nickel, and I led them out to meet their mother after we heard her car in the driveway. "Mommeeeeee!" the little girl I had on my hip screamed when the car door opened.

The mother hurried up our newly neat-and-tidy path. The girl wriggled out of my arms and ran to meet her.

When she was still a few feet away, someone screamed,

"Duck!" which was strange, because there weren't any ducks near our house. Geese, yes; ducks, no.

From somewhere over our heads came a high-pitched whistle. Something small and black hurtled through the sky. It spiraled toward me, twisting as I tried to jump aside. Narrowly missing my head, it looped away and lodged in the side of our house with an almighty crash and the snap of splintering wood.

Nickel bolted across the lawn and didn't stop until he was almost at the gate.

"Was that the satellite?" I yelled, kind of hoping it was, since I was still alive.

"Did you see that?" Mom ran across the lawn to grab me. "That thing went straight for you, Bob, like someone aimed it right at your head."

Nickel pointed with a shaky hand. "When you ducked, it ducked too."

I could not answer, thanks to the shock. Now a missile wanted me dead?

Jared Winkelmeier ran, panting, into our yard. "Oh-my-gosh-I-am-so-sorry!" He bent over and grabbed his knees while he caught his breath. I stared up at the black cylinder poking out from the boards above my bedroom window. Fresh boards that were only months old.

I jabbed my finger through the air at him. "What did you aim that thing at me for?"

Jared, a fourteen-year-old amateur physicist, looked

up at me, face all contorted as he gasped for air. "It's a—rocket—I made for—science fair. It's not meant to travel—this far—or be—that powerful. You can't—even aim it."

"It sure looked like you could," Mom said, her arms wrapped around me. I wasn't sure if it was because she thought the rocket might have hit me, or because she wanted to keep herself from committing acts of vicious sarcasm on Jared Winkelmeier. "It nearly took her head clean off. At least it could have hit one of the places that needed boards replaced. Are people deliberately trying to hit our house now?"

"I'll pay for—the damage, of course," Jared said between gasps.

"Darn right you will, buddy!" I said, wagging a finger at him. "You should be . . ."

I gave up mid-sentence. It wasn't Jared's fault, and I knew it. Bad luck caused this, and possibly some sort of curse that had it in for our house.

Or did it?

What if the curse was on me?

Could the things have been aimed at me all that time? Mrs. Cuthbert's tree had landed on our house, but it had hit my room and my headquarters. I shaded my eyes and stared up at the roof above my room. It had a thick covering of toys, way more than on any other part of the roof.

"No," I whispered. "It couldn't be."

"What couldn't be?" Mom asked, hugging me a bit tighter.

I shook my head, hard, because I needed more time to think. "It doesn't matter."

• • •

Nickel stayed for dinner that night. We sat in front of the television, trying to hear the news preview over the hammering outside, where Jared and his father were patching the hole in the house. Every bang set my nerves further on edge. The satellite was closer than ever, and the house was attracting things like never before. Or I was.

I had to know what was going on with the satellite.

While we waited for the news to start, Mom went to collect sewing supplies from her workroom, and Grandma picked herbs for dinner. I took the chance to ask Nickel the question I'd wanted to ask all evening.

"Has NASA replied to your email yet?"

He glanced up at the clock over the stove. "What time does the six o'clock news start?"

"Six o'clock, obviously. Have you heard from NASA?" I elbowed him, a little harder than I meant to.

He grabbed his ribs and glared at me. "What was that for?"

Narrowing my eyes, I said, "It should be an easy answer. Yes or no."

"Yes," he said. But it didn't seem like any sort of an easy answer. He looked down at his beat-up sneakers as they kicked the edge of Mom's frayed rug.

"What? When? What did they say?" I leaned forward in my chair.

He squirmed around to get a piece of paper from his back pocket and passed it to me. I folded it flat on my thigh to read it.

Dear Mr. Bugden,

Thank you for your letter regarding the decommissioning and reentry of satellite XR-26.

Here at NASA we value public safety above all else. Please rest assured that our calculations indicate it's unlikely the satellite will land anywhere near you.

Best wishes,
Barry Cardogan,
NASA Public Relations

That was it? No plan, no protection, no nothing? I stared at the note until the news started. As usual, the satellite was the first story.

"NASA confirmed the date the defunct XR-26 satellite is predicted to reenter Earth's atmosphere. Public Relations Manager Barry Cardogan had this to say," said the news anchor with a stern look on his face.

Barry Cardogan only had hair around the very edges of his head, and even that was pretty thin. His bright red cheeks were squeezed into a serious expression. "At this stage it is estimated the satellite will reenter Earth's atmosphere on or about June fourteenth. Once again, this is an estimation only."

June fourteenth? Two weeks away.

I tried to send angry brain waves at Barry Cardogan through the TV. It didn't look like he felt them, though. He'd be home with his family constructing an underground bunker by now. Meanwhile, the satellite would put a big halt on my summer before it even began, and on my everything else.

"You know," I said, scrunching the NASA email into a ball, "I am starting to lose faith in adults." I folded my arms across my chest and plopped back in the chair.

"Maybe you should move in with us for a while," Nickel said.

We glanced at each other, and I squeezed the balled-up piece of paper tighter in my hand. "Knowing my luck, your house would just get flattened instead of mine. I'm doomed, and I'm not even a teenager."

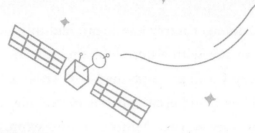

CHAPTER 21

When the phone rang on Monday night, we were in the middle of a Scrabble game. Mom answered, because no one ever called unless it was one of her clients. I figured they must have had a lot to talk about, because it took her a long time to come back from the hallway. Long enough for me to have checked every one of her tiles and have my strategy worked out for the next few moves. Not that I'd do such a thing. Probably.

Mom appeared in the doorway, frowning.

"It's for you, Bob," she said.

Me? The phone was never for me. Nickel had a phone phobia, and no one else had anything to say to me. Except one person.

I jumped up, knocking my tiles onto the floor. *Dad?*

Mom grimaced. "It's someone from that TV show *What's Current.* They want to talk to you about the satellite, of all things."

"It's about time one of us got famous," said Grandma. "Never figured on it being Sparkles, though."

My insides did a little somersault as I ran to the phone.

"Hello, Robyn Goodfellow speaking." Boy, I sure sounded weird when I talked on the phone. Lack of practice, most likely.

"Hi there, Robyn. My name is Felicity Kildare. I'm a reporter for *What's Current*. You've heard of the show, I take it?" She sure sounded like every TV reporter ever—bright, cheerful, and pronouncing every syllable with care.

I nodded before I realized she couldn't see me. "Um, yes."

"Marvelous! I bet you're wondering how I came to have your number."

"Uh-huh," I said.

"We were planning on doing a special-interest piece about the anxiety the satellite is causing, and when we asked around town, your name kept coming up." Felicity Thingamabob chuckled prettily on the other end of the line. That irritated me. I was not anxious. That made it sound like I had nothing to be scared about, and I did. Besides, what I had was more of a slow-burning terror than anxiety.

The reporter continued. "Apparently your house is famous for things landing on the roof, and people are joking the satellite might too."

Joking? Everyone in Calliope thought the satellite

159

would hit us now? I shuddered at that, but I couldn't be sure if it was the eeriness of having the whole town think we were doomed, or if I was seething so hard it made me shake.

"Yes. Everything hits my house." I tried to sound polite instead of ticked off.

"And you think the satellite will too?"

I shivered again. "Yes."

The reporter chuckled again. "Oh dear. Never mind. I'm sure it will all turn out just fine. I would love it if you would talk to me on camera about your concerns and how this whole satellite thing is affecting you. Would that be okay? Your mother said she didn't mind. That it was up to you."

Her voice was the sort toddlers used when trying to scam Mom for extra candy.

The people at NASA weren't interested in helping us. No one believed we were in danger, except all the Calliopeans, apparently. Maybe my going on TV would get NASA's attention, or someone would come up with a plan for how to save us. Or maybe my dad would see the broadcast and come find me. Even if none of that happened, at least I would be remembered.

"Yes," I said.

Felicity Kildare and her crew would be at our house the next day to film. I might only have a couple of weeks left to be famous, but it would be better than nothing.

I sat down in front of my Scrabble tiles, which Mom had put back into their stand. She reached across the board to pat my hand. "You're in a tizzy about this satellite, aren't you?"

When she came out and asked like that, it sounded stupid and unimportant. I felt my cheeks get warm. "Kinda."

She squeezed my fingers. "I know it's scary. It makes me a bit nervous too. But I remind myself how huge this world is and how tiny we are. NASA would do something if they thought it would land on people, and that makes me feel better."

If they were as bad at "doing something" as they were at figuring out satellite trajectories, we were in deep doo-doo. But I only mumbled, "So everyone says."

Leaning over the board and tiles, she pecked my cheek. "Trust me, Robyn Goodfellow. I'll keep you safe. I promise."

I so hoped she was right and all this would turn out okay.

Meanwhile, the next day I would have a chance to talk to someone who had also talked to my other family once.

• • •

"I could come over to watch and make sure you don't say anything embarrassing," Nickel said at lunch the next day. It felt like the first time we had eaten lunch together in forever.

"What makes you think I'll embarrass myself?"

"I'm not going to answer, on the grounds it may get me punched." He grinned and popped a soggy french fry into his mouth.

I wanted to be angry at him, and I gave it a good try, but my enthusiasm wasn't there. I never wanted to lose my best friend again. Before our fight, I never thought I could.

"You can come."

Nickel punched his fist in the air. "Sweet."

We walked home together after school. It would be his second visit to my house in a week. Impending disaster made people do strange things, I guessed. Not to mention what they'd do for a shot at fame.

"Which do you think is my best side?" he asked, jogging backward alongside me. He turned his face one way, then the other.

"Your back side," I said, and giggled.

"Hur, hur, hur. Have you thought about what you're going to say? You don't want to look stupid."

I had thought about it. A lot. In fact, I had a whole speech planned. But I couldn't say it out loud before the interview, or I would lose my nerve.

"Not exactly," I said.

● ● ●

When Nickel and I got home, a van with *What's Current* printed in gold letters on the side was parked out front.

Behind it was a truck with a huge extendable arm like the one on the back of the firetruck when they rescued kitties from our roof.

"That's a cherry picker," Nickel said. "They use it to film high stuff, like the roof. It's awesome. Check out the hydraulics on that thing."

I was suddenly too nervous to think of a reply or even wonder what hydraulics were.

Our entire block was the sort of quiet that a neighborhood could only be when all its occupants were inside, peeping from behind their curtains. My stomach turned into a spaghetti tangle of nerves. Talking to Felicity Kildare the night before on the phone had been fine, but now it was real and terrifying.

"I can't remember anything I wanted to say."

Nickel laughed at me until he saw my face. "Don't worry. It'll be okay. She'll ask questions and you answer them. Make it up."

Make it up?

I was even more doomed than I thought.

Mom and Felicity Kildare sat chatting in the Fairy Wonderland, with Grandma, mostly hidden behind a cross-eyed sheep, watching. The reporter looked exactly like a TV personality—tall, with black hair pulled back into a tight bun, big dark eyes, and makeup so perfect she almost didn't look real. A couple of guys with cameras followed her around. She thrust her hand, full of bright pink fingernails, at me. "You must be Robyn. I'm Felicity Kildare."

I took her hand in my good one and gave it a backward shake. "Hi, Ms. Kildare."

The reporter smiled the neatest and whitest smile I ever saw. "Oh, please, call me Felicity."

Nickel stepped forward and held out his hand. It was the most grown-up thing I had ever seen him do. "Hi, I'm Nickel Bugden, Robyn's best friend."

Felicity shook his hand while still looking at me. It was kind of rude. "What happened to your arm, Robyn?"

I glanced down at the cast. It had a lot more graffiti on it now that Nickel and I were best friends again. "I tripped and broke it. No big deal."

The reporter looked disappointed. "Oh, I thought the rocket your mom told me about on the phone might have hit it." The way she said it made me think she would be happier if it had.

The cameramen worked at attaching cameras and massive spotlights to tripods. Felicity looked around, taking in the wonder that was a fairyland filled with wonky animals.

"This is the perfect place for the interview," she said, taking a seat on one of the papier-mâché toadstools. I perched on another, swiping crepe paper willow fronds away from my face.

Grandma, Mom, and Nickel sat on the rock-shaped

table to watch. I stared into the bright lights, orange patterns appearing on the insides of my lids when I blinked.

Felicity waved her hand in front of my eyes. "We are rolling, Robyn."

I frowned at her. "Rolling what?"

Felicity drew her finger across her throat like she was playing pirate, and sighed. "Let's go again."

She asked all the easy questions first, like name, age, grade, and school. Then she got to the serious stuff. "Tell me why you think the satellite will land on your house, Robyn."

It made sense in my head, but I knew it would sound silly out loud. "It's like our roof has its own personal gravity or something."

I could tell Ms. Kildare wanted to smile, but she hid it well. Squashed kids are hardly funny. "You know the chances of the satellite landing on your house are infinitesimal?"

"So are the chances of a skydiver dangling from our weather vane." I had to work hard at keeping the sarcasm out of my voice. "It still happened."

After I told the story of Nickel's email to NASA, it was his turn. He gave his eyewitness account of the time Sarah-Belle's inflatable My Little Pony ended up dangling from the eaves over my bedroom window. When he was done, it was time to go outside.

The cherry picker truck reversed up our driveway with

a cameraman in the basket. I hoped he would not get high enough to fall from our roof too. The cherry picker whirred and creaked as it wound itself up, up, up for a view of our roof.

The cameraman shouted down, "I could grab a Frisbee or two if you want."

That offer would have been very handy a week earlier. "No, thank you."

He laughed and said something about awesome footage. Felicity's teeth glittered in a delighted smile; they were even brighter in the sunlight and made me glad that my glasses had lenses that got darker outside. After a while, the cherry picker eased back down to the ground, and the cameraman stepped out of the basket.

Next they filmed me waving through the gaping hole in my headquarters and pointing at the spot where Mrs. Cuthbert's tree used to be. We finished on the front lawn with Nickel and me holding up the crumpled email from NASA. If this was fame, it felt an awful lot like posing for a great-aunt on a visit from Canada—except with more questions and less cheek pinching.

Felicity turned to the camera. "Thank you, Robyn and Nickel. And come on, NASA, there is still time. Help a girl out, won't you?"

Felicity smiled and waited a few seconds before saying, "And cut." She thanked us all as she shook our hands again. "The interview should be on tomorrow evening's broadcast. I'm sure you'll love it!" The men began to dismantle their cameras and load boxes of gear into the back of the van.

"Wait," I said. "I have something else to say."

The reporter's grin faded a bit as she glanced at her watch. "It will have to be fast. David?"

One of the cameramen hoisted the smallest camera onto his shoulder and pointed it at me.

"I have a special message." I swallowed hard and glanced at Grandma, who was setting her rosebushes free. Hopefully, she was too busy to listen in. I couldn't see where Mom had gotten to, but I knew I'd have to take the risk. Keeping my voice as low as I could, I said, "If my dad is watching, I want him to know I'm a pretty good kid, and I want to meet him before the satellite hits. Benjamin O'Malley, contact me while there is still time. Thank you."

Felicity blinked. "Wait . . . O'Malley. How do I know that name?"

I reminded her about the report she had done—the albino kids and the picnic—and told her about Benjamin O'Malley. Her eyes got very wide. "Oh, you poor kid. You're much too well behaved to be one of them."

Parts of me got hot and angry at that comment. What was so wrong with my family, anyway—apart from the obvious things, like magnet roofs and Michael?

"You and I have to talk," Felicity said, resting a hand on my shoulder and directing me toward the van.

Grandma stepped between us, a sprig of accidentally broken rosebush in her hand. Her eyes were bright and wild. My heart made a sharp jump in my chest. Had she heard every word?

Grandma put her hand on my arm. "Thank you for your time, Ms. Kildare, but I can handle this from here. Nickel, time for you to skedaddle off home."

Before I had a chance to protest, Grandma herded me inside and locked the door behind us.

"Grandma, I—"

"Sofa. Then we talk."

My heart was a speedy tickle in my chest. Mom would find out what I had said. I might be grounded for life. But if my father heard my message on TV and came looking for me, it would be worth it. I sat down on the comfy part of the sofa while Grandma pulled the coffee table closer and perched on the edge of it.

"Tell me everything," she said.

It was too late to hide anything now. Besides, if my plan worked, Dad would come find me. If it didn't, then telling Grandma couldn't make things any worse. So I told her everything.

She listened to my story without interrupting once, which is a special Grandma-only superpower. When it was over, I held my breath, waiting for the lecture, or the grounding, or worse. She was quiet a long time, staring at the messages on my cast as if they had more of my secrets to tell.

At last, she patted her knees and sighed. "We sure have missed a lot."

She nodded once, almost to herself, then stood and went upstairs.

I had not seen that coming and didn't have the first clue what to do next. I sat frozen for a long time, eventually turning on the TV when she didn't come back. The clock ticked on and on without any sign of her or Mom.

By bedtime, I thought I might be worried—or annoyed—but mostly I was hungry.

We hadn't even had dinner.

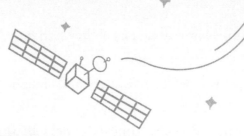

CHAPTER 22

Nickel was late to school the next morning. I had to tell him about Grandma's weirdness during Mrs. Gilbert's class or wait until lunchtime. A note was too risky, so I came up with a better idea. Holding my cast under my desk, I scrawled a note across the palm section, where Mrs. Gilbert would think it was just another autograph.

Grandma knows I tried to find Dad. Mom will hate me now.

I made a small coughing sound so that Nickel would glance over at me, and I passed him an eraser. Staring hard at my palm, I spread my fingers wide, hoping he would get the idea.

He did not.

But Mrs. Gilbert did.

"Aha! I see what you did there," she said, striding between the desks toward me.

The class got silent, and all their faces turned toward me, most of them grinning in anticipation of a juicy new entry in the school newspaper. At least Dameon looked a tiny bit sympathetic. He'd provided more notes for the school paper than anyone else, ever.

Nickel's eyes widened in horror as the teacher took my hand and spread out my fingers to see my note. I tried to pull away, but I couldn't put up much of a fight with a cast.

Everyone would laugh. Worse, everyone would know what a reject I'd been all my life.

The satellite could crush me now and I wouldn't care, especially if it opened up a giant hole in the earth for me to fall into.

"I'll just write this down for the paper, shall . . ." The teacher's voice trailed off as she read the note. Her lips turned into a thin line, and her head hung a little bit. "Never mind. I—I guess I was mistaken. Back to work, kids. Those assignments are due in a few days." As she turned to walk away, her hand hovered for a moment over my shoulder.

I screwed my eyes closed and rested my forehead on my desk. Whatever Mrs. Gilbert knew about my mom and dad, I wasn't sure I wanted to know it anymore.

• • •

Nickel came over to watch our television debut. While we waited for *What's Current* to start, we discussed Grandma

171

in whispers. We had not seen her since we arrived. Or Mom. In fact, I had barely seen either of them since the night before.

"Are you in trouble, or what?" Nickel asked.

I shrugged. "I don't know. I kind of wish I was. This is . . . creepy."

Grandma showed up just before the opening credits played. She sat down on the uncomfortable-spring end of the sofa and leaned forward on her elbows to watch. Nickel and I sat up straight and barely breathed, waiting for her to do something. There was no sign of Mom.

The interview needed to get Benjamin O'Malley's attention, because this much awkward could not be for nothing.

On the screen, Felicity Kildare and several of her co-workers stood with their arms crossed, staring meaning-fully at the audience as the titles rolled. She looked a lot more impressive all serious-faced and lit from behind.

Our story was first up, and the screen switched to Felicity's smiling face.

"I'm here on Pinetree Lane in the heart of Calliope with Robyn Goodfellow—a girl with a big problem. Robyn lives in a house with a knack for attracting falling objects. The roof of her family home is littered with toys and remote-controlled flying objects. So many, in fact, that our Eye in the Sky traffic helicopter tells me the house is something of a local landmark. Not surprisingly, the news that a satellite is heading our way has Robyn a little anxious." While Felicity spoke, the camera cut away to shots of the things on our roof.

I gasped and grabbed Nickel's arm. Even I had not realized how much was up there, especially around my room.

"It's like a Toys'R'Us exploded on our house," I said.

"Nah. They had a few bags of toys to add up there to make it look good on TV. The Eye in the Sky doesn't even fly over here," Nickel said. I hoped he was right and not just trying to make me feel better.

The next shot was of me waving from the giant hole in the side of my headquarters.

"Early this year, their neighbor cut down her tree, only to have it defy all the laws of physics and land on Robyn's tree house and bedroom window, simultaneously."

The camera cut to a close-up shot of my face. "I had to sleep on the sofa for ages," I said with a serious expression. "It's got a wonky spring in it too."

"Another collision occurred recently when a neighbor's science fair experiment crashed into the wall—right into Robyn's own bedroom." The camera focused on the newest patch, in the middle of the slightly older tree patch above my window.

"It's like the house has its own gravity," I said solemnly. Nickel and Grandma both cracked up at that, which was not very kind, although it was good to hear Grandma laugh. I wished Mom was there too, preferably laughing along with us.

The next shot was of Felicity and me inside the Fairy Wonderland, surrounded by nervous-looking woodland creatures. "Robyn, what would you like to see happen?"

"I want NASA to put some sort of shield over my house. It's their satellite. It's worse than littering. It's . . . irresponsible."

The clip finished outside with Nickel and me holding NASA's email and looking uncomfortable while Felicity read the text aloud. "Thank you, Robyn and Nickel. And come on, NASA, there is still time. Help a girl out, won't you?"

When it was over, Grandma let out a sigh that sounded relieved. "That's that, then."

I tried to think of something to say, even something that would make her mad. But before I could, she stood up and left. A few seconds later, her feet thudded and creaked on their way up the stairs.

Nickel and I glanced at each other. He mouthed, "Huh?" as we waited for Grandma's footsteps to fade out. When she was gone, he looked at me with wide eyes. "Okay, that was strange."

"I know. She's totally weirding me out," I whispered.

"They didn't play the bit about your dad."

"I know that too."

Grandma and Mom hated me, and I had done it all for nothing.

• • •

The local gossips—which meant pretty much everyone—telephoned to talk to us before school. Sometimes it seemed like all they were saying was goodbye, just in case. Mom didn't come down for breakfast, and I began to think that maybe I'd broken her somehow. Grandma could not get me out of the house fast enough. Every neighbor between our house and school peeked through their curtains to watch me run by. I didn't stop until I met Nickel outside the school gates.

"The whole town has gone super creepy," I said, bending over to catch my breath.

"Don't worry. Kids don't watch the news," Nickel said as we walked into school.

"We did," I said.

"We were on it. That's different."

That made me feel a little better until we reached our lockers. There, stuck to my locker door, was a hand-drawn arrow pointing downward with a sign that read HERE SHE IS, XR-26. Out of sight, someone giggled—someone who sounded a whole lot like Dameon Swenson. Nickel reached out to snatch the paper, but I stopped him.

"No. Leave it." Gritting my teeth, I stalked off toward our first class.

"Uh, why?" Nickel asked, hurrying along beside me.

"Because it's true. Because I don't care who laughs at me. Just because."

Except I did care. Very much. I would have smashed that satellite right out of the sky and onto Dameon Swenson's head if my arms had been long enough. The bad karma would be so worth it.

Nickel sat with me all day for support. Everyone else kept at least six feet between me and them, even moving their desks and chairs away as if bad luck or magnet roofs might be contagious. At lunchtime, Nickel and I sat in our favorite spot and tried to ignore the pointing and whispering and new table layout.

Nickel picked up a weird lump of brown dough from his tray and turned it around in his fingers. "Do you think this is a cinnamon roll? I can't tell if it's meat or dessert."

I pinched off a bite and tasted it. "No idea. It could go either way."

We giggled for the first time all day. After a few minutes, people quit staring and got on with their food and friends. Things felt better, almost normal, until Darren Morse sidled up to our table.

"I saw my RC helicopter on your roof on TV last night," he said. "I want it back."

No "please." No "thank you." No "How's your doughnut or possibly meat loaf?"

"You're welcome to climb up there and get it," I said.

176

His eyes bulged like a frog's. "You get it down. You stole it. Mrs. Cuthbert says it's theft. She told my mom your whole family should be arrested, not put on television."

Everyone in the room stared at us, frozen in mid-chew.

The thing about kids like Darren Morse was that they were born with so many genes for stupidity, you could not win an argument with them, because they'd never know they lost.

"Then sue my roof."

"Yeah. You're bound to win, since you're taking your legal advice from a secret FBI agent," Nickel said. The sarcasm was so perfect all the kids in the cafeteria burst out laughing.

Darren's neck turned a deep scarlet that spread upward until it reached the top of his head. "Thieves!" he yelled, and stamped off.

When we were alone again, Nickel grinned. "Admit it. We handled that like Focus Pocus masters."

I laughed. "Yeah. We crushed his tiny little spirit."

Later Nickel sat beside me in class, looking like he might fall asleep on his books at any second. I leaned over to whisper while Mrs. Cooper wrote math equations on the board, her chalk screeching, hopefully covering my whispers. "I have a new plan."

Nickel raised an eyebrow at me. He'd practiced that trick for months and finally had the hang of it. "What now?"

"Your mom takes Penny to Densdale for her ballet lessons tonight, right?" I whispered.

He held his finger to his lips. "Shhh! People would flip if they knew the cop's wife took her kid to Densdale instead of Madam Shallot's."

"Sorry. Anyway, we could go too."

Nickel sighed and rested his face in his hands. "No. No. No."

"Why not?"

"I'm not asking. Mom would say no."

I made a *pfft* sound. "So? When it comes to grown-ups, 'no' is the first step in a long process."

"Let it go. It's over. Forget about it."

"What, I'm supposed to wait quietly and accept my fate?"

Nickel nodded. "That would be a nice change."

Angry heat spread over my skin. Not Nickel too. Not again. I needed him on my side. "Just me, then. I'll escape when I get there."

"Nickel Bugden and Robyn Goodfellow, eyes on books and mouths shut, please."

Nickel turned green and sank in his seat. He stared at the board and ignored me.

I tugged at his sleeve. "Please. It's my last chance. There's no more time."

He shook his head.

Breathing through my teeth, I clenched my fists hard enough to leave deep little nail prints in my palms. "Don't do this to me."

He turned to glare at me and said, way too loud, "No!"

That was how we earned our first detention.

• • •

Mrs. Cooper had taught my mom when she was at school. She'd probably taught Grandma too. Everything about Mrs. Cooper was gray. She looked like one of the ornaments on the bookshelf that Grandma never dusted.

When all the other classrooms in Calliope Middle School had their old chalkboards swapped for giant dry-erase boards and markers, Mrs. Cooper refused to change. She still used the same textbooks and lesson plans she'd always followed. And the same punishments. Her classroom was like a museum dedicated to last century's schools.

Neither Nickel nor I had ever been in detention before, much less detention with Mrs. Cooper, but everyone in school knew her routine. We sat in silence, staring at the top of the teacher's head as she bent over a pile of papers at her desk.

I sucked my dry lips into my mouth as she slowly raised her head, like she had finally noticed we were there.

"These tasks must be completed to my satisfaction before you may go home," she said. "The blackboard must be washed down until not a single streak remains, and the erasers taken outside and cleared of their dust. You may begin."

Nickel and I looked at each other. "Board first?" he asked.

I nodded and followed him to the front of the classroom. Mrs. Cooper pointed to a pile of rags and a bucket by the sink under the windows. We wet our rags and started to wash.

The thing about chalkboards was that they looked lovely and black and clean while they were wet, but the minute they dried, they were nothing but chalky streaks. We got to the end of the huge board and realized we would have to start all over again with a fresh bucket of water.

What was so wrong with dry-erase boards, anyway? They were good enough for every other teacher in the entire universe and needed zero scrubbing—which was probably the whole point.

"It looks good this time," I said as I stood back at the end of our second pass.

"Uh, not so much." Nickel pointed back at the start, where the board had dried. There were almost as many streaks as on the last pass.

Mrs. Cooper chuckled to herself at her desk but kept reading her papers.

We went back to the sink and refilled the bucket. It took

five passes before we had the board streak-free and up to Mrs. Cooper's standards. Water from the rags dribbled down my good arm.

"There are eight erasers. Four each. Off you go." Mrs. Cooper pointed at the dusters sitting on the wooden ledge under the board.

Since my cast did not allow for smacking wooden erasers together, I carried them all stacked in my arms. Nickel banged the felt sides of the first two dusters together, sending clouds of pink and white chalk dust into the air. A couple of times, he stopped and opened his mouth like he wanted to say something, then closed it again. I hoped that whatever he wanted to say came in the form of an apology for getting us detention.

Summer was close in Calliope, and that day the sun shone like it wanted to make up for lost time, sucking all the wet out of the ground and turning everything sticky and miserable. Without even a light breeze to carry the chalk dust away, it stuck to our skin and turned our mouths gummy and dry. By the time the first erasers ran out of chalk dust, the powder clung to my sunscreened skin in colorful smears and streaks.

Instead of driving to Densdale with Mrs. Bugden, we were filthy and cranky, wasting what little time I had left. But I'd only had my best friend back for a few days, and I'd learned my lesson about putting satellites and fathers before our friendship. That didn't mean I had to like it, though.

We were almost finished when Nickel stopped pounding erasers and looked at me. He took a deep breath. "I can't stand it anymore. There's something I have to tell you."

He pointed at the steps outside the classroom. "You better sit down."

Uh-oh. The only words that worried me worse than "There's something I have to tell you" were "You better sit down."

CHAPTER 23

I sat down on the concrete steps outside Mrs. Cooper's classroom and wrapped my arms around my knees. Nickel looked guilty and a bit shaky, which didn't make me feel any better.

He took a deep breath and went for it. "When you and your grandma went inside after the filming of *What's Current,* Felicity Kildare and I talked. I wanted to tell you what she said, but I didn't know how."

Even in the sunshine, the little hairs on my good arm stood up. "What did she say?"

"She said the other kids are all like Michael, out of control. You're the only nice one. If that's true, can you imagine how bad they are?"

I could have been insulted, but I knew he was right.

"That's not all. She said that she'd met Benjamin O'Malley before too, on another story about men who'd come home from the war. He got hurt and traumatized.

He's . . . well, she said he probably wouldn't remember your mom, or about you."

It was too late now to decide I didn't want to hear it.

Nickel reached out and held my shoulders, all stiff and awkward. "Unless your mom tells you about him or he goes for blood tests or whatever they do, you won't get any answers. Even if you met him, I don't think he'd be able to do any of the things you want him to do."

I wanted to be angry at Nickel. For this news. For ruining my father. But I couldn't.

"They were just some random family Felicity Kildare met," I said. "She wouldn't remember him that well. It could have been any of them. Or maybe he's not my dad, and one of the others is."

"Do you really think that?" Nickel's voice got all gentle.

"Well, it could be. It could be that he was pretending. It could be anything. . . ." I stopped, because I knew it wasn't anything. Alyssa had said in the car that he wasn't the same since fighting overseas. It had to be the same Benjamin O'Malley.

My eyes felt hot and my nose ran, but I couldn't let myself cry. If I did, Mrs. Cooper would want to know why, and I had no more lies left. I had wasted them all on a father who never wanted me and wouldn't know me now, even if he changed his mind.

My cousins, or relatives, or whatever, weren't worth finding either. They were all horrible. Every one of them, except me. It was just another way I didn't fit in, even in the one place where it should have been easy.

"You don't need him," Nickel said. "You really don't. I can help. I—I've been coming over as often as I can so I can protect you if the satellite comes. He couldn't do any better than me. And your name is just fine. It's awesome, and it suits you. And Puck wasn't a silly fairy—he was a cool one. I read the whole story. Trust me. It's a great name."

I looked at Nickel and blinked. "You've been coming over to look out for me?"

He nodded and stared down at his dusty fingers. "Don't get all full of yourself or anything."

Despite everything, I smiled.

Mrs. Cooper called us inside, but I didn't move. Nickel held out his hand to help me up, hauled me to my feet, and led me inside.

"C'mon. It's time to go home."

. . .

As soon as I reached our driveway, I felt a little better. I was home. At least I still had that.

I jumped over the roses and headed inside.

Maybe Mom had heard me before I arrived, because when I flung the door open, she was there, waiting. Small, with ridiculously big green eyes and a relieved sort of smile.

Grandma stood in the Fairy Wonderland doorway, not

smiling much at all. "Come in and sit down, both of you. We can talk in the living room."

Talk? So this was it. Grounded for eternity.

The kitchen smelled buttery and delicious. Grandma baked when she got stressed. My stomach had gurgled the whole way home from school, but my appetite had left the moment I saw how serious their faces were.

For the second time that day, someone said, "There's something I have to tell you." At least I was already sitting down when Mom said it.

She was staring at her hands, which were folded on her lap.

"Oh?" I asked, doing a pretty good impression of a girl who hadn't done anything wrong, which I technically was if you didn't count the detention, snooping through Mom's things, and a sneaky trip to Densdale in a rickshaw.

"You've been trying to find your father, haven't you?" Mom closed her eyes and took a deep breath. For a split second I thought of making a run for it.

If she'd asked me the day before, I probably could have lied. But today was different, because now I knew that my father was not the dad I'd thought he was; he was just a bunch of memories in a jar.

My lip trembled, even though I bit down hard to make it stop. "Don't worry, Mom. It doesn't matter anymore. He wouldn't know me or want me anyway."

"We realize that you think you know all about your dad. We had a visitor this morning," Grandma said. "Alyssa O'Malley. She saw you on TV and came to find to us."

"I'm sorry, Mom," I whispered.

Mom's face softened a bit, which made things much worse. "Don't be. I should have talked about all this a very long time ago, but I wasn't ready. I am now."

I looked up, curiosity beating out everything else. Even though I knew almost all of it, I wanted to hear it from her.

"I haven't always been totally honest with you, Bob." Of all the secrets she could have told, that was the least surprising. I had known that even before the O'Malleys came along. After another deep breath, she carried on. "You know how I told you that your dad left us, and I hadn't heard from him since?"

"Sure."

Her forehead wrinkled. "What I said is true, sort of, but not entirely. He—he was gone, and I decided it would be better if you thought you had a mysterious dad who'd left us. . . ."

"Because he didn't want me?" I finished for her. It was like someone had sprayed me with father repellent. "Because he probably doesn't even remember us? I know."

"No, Bob, you don't know at all. He never even got to meet you." She rested her hand on her belly. "All he knew was a tiny little bump. And he wanted to be your dad very much."

I thought of the card in her mason jar. My father had seemed to want me when he wrote it. But why had he written that and then left us? All of this had made sense to me the day before, but now I had no idea what was true anymore. "I don't understand."

For a second, I thought she had nothing else to say. Her smile was weak and sad. "I know you think your dad was called Benjamin O'Malley, but that's not him. His name was Byron. He was an actor. We met when we were both cast in *A Midsummer Night's Dream* at the Majestic in Densdale. I was Titania, he was Puck. That's why I—"

"Named me Robyn Goodfellow."

"Yes. And your names are connected too. Robyn and Byron, same letters, different order. Robyn and Robin Goodfellow/Puck. Plus, his last name was Goode, so that worked too. We never got a chance to marry. I thought I would change our name to Goodfellow, because it seemed almost like naming you after him. Do you see?"

My whole life made a kind of sense it never had before. "Benjamin O'Malley isn't my dad?"

Mom shook her head. "I'm impressed with how you came to the conclusion he was, though."

Resting my chin on my hands, I closed my eyes to process everything. Now I knew why Mom obsessed about fairies, why she hadn't wanted me to study the play, and why she'd named me Robyn. It was still awful, but in a completely different way than it had been an hour earlier.

I also had a mother with a very flimsy relationship with the truth. On the bright side, I had no genetic connection to Michael at all.

What I didn't understand was why she had never let me meet my real father. Where was he now?

"Anything else I should know?" I had to work hard not to sound angry or upset or sad, because I wanted her to keep talking. We had never talked like this in my whole life about anything to do with my father.

Mom tried on a shaky grin. "He was an ordinary but wonderful man with curly copper hair and icicle-blue eyes. You look so much like him, but pale. Almost like his ghost."

I touched my hair and smiled. I'd been compared to a ghost before as an insult, but this was the first time it seemed like a good thing, like it made me more real, more me. "Can I meet him? I could find him if you don't know where he is. It turns out I'm pretty good at that sort of thing."

Mom put a finger to her lips to hush me. "Listen. I wanted more than anything for you to meet your dad. But he's gone." She took a deep, shuddering breath, and I realized she didn't mean he had moved away. Without her saying anything or sharing any more secrets, I knew what had happened. And it was the worst thing ever.

"One day, he was rehearsing the play. I was home, resting up for the performance the next day. Your dad was onstage, practicing his final speech. The lighting tech was up in the rigging, adjusting the setup." Mom swiped a tear away from under her eye with her thumb. "A lighting can fell. They're big. Weigh a lot. So, that was that."

My heart had gone absolutely still in my chest. "He died because something fell on him?"

Mom nodded, holding the hem of her sleeve under her nose.

I had to grip the edge of the chair to keep from swaying. My father was dead. I would never meet him, no matter how much I planned or how many ways I found to get to Densdale. Nothing I did would take me far enough.

But that wasn't all.

Something else made sense now. Something huge and terrifying.

Our roof wasn't magnetic or a klepto-thingamabob.

I was.

Now I knew it for certain. Things landed on our roof because I was under it.

My father had died because something fell on him. I was genetically predisposed, just like with albinism and icicle-blue eyes and springy hair.

Mom's chair scraped as she stood up. "Are you okay?"

"Mom, did things fall on our house before I was born?"

"Once in a while, I suppose. I don't remember. Momma, what do you think?"

Grandma, who had not said a word through all this, took a sip from her dainty cup of tea. "I don't think so. It's a recent thing. Kids didn't have so many newfangled flying toys in my day."

They had kites, though. They had balls. They had plenty of things that could have found their way onto our roof even back then. A horrible shiver wriggled its way through my body. I wanted to get up and run away. Where would be far enough? Where could I go that the satellite wouldn't be able to find me?

Mom put her arms around my shoulders. "Oh, baby. Even if the satellite did come down in Calliope, there are a million places it might land other than here."

I managed to control my shakes but got a whopping case of hiccups for my trouble. "Even the newspeople think it's going to happen, or they wouldn't bother filming us." *Hic.* "Have you ever looked properly at our roof? It was my room the stupid tree landed on." *Hic.* "My room and my headquarters. It's me things land on, not the house."

Ever since the first news broadcast about the satellite, even when I'd concentrated on finding my dad, I had been scared, even very scared sometimes, but not quite terrified. Now, as Mom hugged me tight, I was. I so was.

She took my face in her hands. "I want you to listen to me. The area where NASA estimates the satellite will land is huge. Beyond huge. So far beyond huge it's like floating a leaf in the middle of Lake Erie and trying to throw a stone to hit it."

The odds of being born with albinism or having a lighting can fall on your dad's head or a tree land on your bedroom had to be almost as tiny. Look how that had turned out.

"But it's possible you could hit it, right?" I said. "It could happen, and you can't swear and promise it won't. And if that leaf was genetically destined to be hit by a flying stone, the chances would go up and up."

Mom's face twitched a bit as she tried not to smile, which was plain rude of her under the circumstances. "There is no such thing as a genetic destiny for something like that. Besides, I'm your mother, and things don't fall on me."

Except she was only half of my parents. Now did not seem like the right time to remind her of that, though. I had gotten an awful lot of the things that made me *me* from my dad. *My* dad. Byron Goode.

Grandma put down the plate of chocolate fairy's-food cake she had been eating and pointed her fork at the TV. "Someone turn the sound up. It's a newsflash about the satellite."

CHAPTER 24

After everything I had learned about my dad, it was hard to switch my brain to concentrate on the television. I did my best to focus as the special-bulletin theme finished.

Barry Cardogan—world's least accurate satellite forecaster—cleared his throat and said, "It would appear the satellite will make landfall in approximately the next ten days or so, around the fourteenth of June, as predicted earlier. We feel that the most likely landing zone is between twenty-five and fifty-five degrees north latitude."

"Where does that zone fall in North America?" the reporter asked him.

"From the middle of Canada to the southern tip of Florida. But the satellite could fall anywhere within that zone around the globe."

Ten more days.

Felicity Kildare phoned within minutes of the broadcast's ending. This time, Mom spoke to her. After she hung up, the phone rang again. In fact, it rang and rang until Mom swore at it and took it off the hook. I watched her, my eyes bulging until they made my skull ache. She turned around slowly and gave me a wobbly smile.

"This doesn't mean anything. That area is practically the whole of the Northern Hemisphere," she said, clearly not believing it herself. "But just in case, we'll pack up Grandma's car and go on vacation in Wisconsin, won't we, Momma?"

Considering how far away Wisconsin is, Mom obviously thought it did mean something.

Grandma nodded. "Sure we will. We can make a week of it. Picnic, hike, fishing. Whatever."

"That's a nice idea," I said, "but it won't matter if it's me the satellite is after. We'd have to drive to Mexico City to be sure."

"Then we'll go to Mexico City. It's about time we had a break," Mom said. "We could fly down."

"Really?" I asked, feeling relief, sweet and cool, run through my body. Maybe I had a future after all, even if it would be a homeless one.

"Sure," Grandma said. "We couldn't go till the week after that, though. We're booked solid for parties till then."

The lovely cool feeling dried up into something cold and sickening. "Oh."

"There's still a bit of time," Mom said. "We'll see what we can do."

That night Mom tucked me in, taking extra-special care and sitting on the edge of my bed to stroke the curls away from my eyes. Cradled in her other arm was her mason jar treasure chest. I did my best not to look at it, but I couldn't help myself.

She left a delicate little kiss on the tip of my nose. "I promise I shall not lie to you again."

I rolled my eyes, because we both knew how bad she was at promises.

With a sad smile, she tapped the lid of the jar. "I have some things here. Things from your dad that I thought you might like to see. I have some other things too, in that suitcase I put in storage. I'll bring it home for you soon."

Nodding, I sat back and waited while she unscrewed the lid and carefully took out each treasure, one at a time. I held my breath, waiting to see if she could tell that the things had been touched, but if she could, she didn't let on.

She showed me the notes and the card and explained the story behind each of them. I forgot the glimpses I'd seen, because they were all brand-new when Mom talked about them. Then, once the lid had been screwed back on, she took something out of the pocket of her shirt. A photo.

My heart did a big double thump, and I couldn't look anywhere else.

Mom held the photo out to me. "That's your dad and me together."

On the back, it read *Byron and Mary*. I flipped it over, biting my lip hard. At last I would know what he looked like.

He was tall, pretty good-looking, but not as much like me as I'd hoped he would be. Not albino, but most parents of kids with albinism just carried the gene. One thing stood out, though: his tightly curled, very red hair. In fact, he looked more like Nickel than like me.

That made me smile. "Thank you, Mom." I wrapped my arms around her neck and hugged her tight.

Her smile was sad. "I'm sorry I didn't show you years ago. I know I should have. It's not fair to you or to him. His own daughter should know about him. He would have been miserable to think I never mentioned him anymore, especially to you."

"It's going to be all right now, though."

I looked at the picture one last time and held it out for her, but she didn't take it. "You can keep it. I have a scan on my computer."

I propped the photo up on my nightstand against my treasure chest and stared at it some more. Now I had a face and a name, and it all added up to a real dad—even if everything left of him was kept in a jar under my mother's cabinet.

Mom stood up slowly, like her muscles ached. "Sleep well, Bob. We'll talk more another time, okay?"

"Okay," I said. "Night, Mom."

She turned to leave, but I stopped her. "Mom, one last thing," I said. "Wear your wings tomorrow, okay?"

She laughed and flitted through the door. Her face lit up with her best, most real smile, and she looked like my mom again. "Absolutely."

After she'd gone, I opened *A Midsummer Night's Dream* and began to read it for real. My dad had practiced and read those lines, and I could read them too. Maybe an ice cream date was out of the question, but there were still things we could share. Like the play, and springy hair, and my name, which had been so perfect all along.

I'd never have my actual dad, but I'd always have my mom, and that was pretty great, even if I didn't like the chances of her getting me an iguana.

But how long would I have her? Until the fourteenth of June?

I had found my dad, but I still had to face the satellite.

I stared up at the glowing stars on my ceiling, imagining a streak of bright light heading straight for me. It would explode in a blast of heat and splintered house, and there I would be, a pancake underneath it.

Now I knew how the dinosaurs had felt.

Every night for the next week, the news reports got worse and Calliope got a bit stranger—which was not easy, considering where it had started out. People sold commemorative coffee mugs and hard hats, and some smarty-pants spray-painted a giant bull's-eye target in the middle of our front lawn while we slept. My heart did little flip-flops every time I saw it.

People emptied the shelves in the supermarket. I guessed they were worried the satellite would land on the shops and they would be forced to forage in Densdale for supplies.

Whenever I went out, people nudged each other, gave me pitying glances, or stepped a few feet away, just in case. One lady even whipped out her phone to take a selfie with me. Another had me sign her grocery receipt. I guessed it would make her a fortune online once I got squished.

Mr. Parker, our other neighbor, worked in his front yard during the evenings, bending over an old-fashioned shovel or using a pickax to dig out rocks. He had barely made a dent in the stony earth. He wiped a heavy work glove over his forehead and glared at us as I helped Mom hang paper fairies from the porch beams. Mom had decided to go over the top on fairy stuff until things felt right again.

"Laying in a new garden, Mr. Parker?" Mom asked,

teetering on the third step of Grandma's ancient step-ladder.

He scuffed the dirt and dried grass with his shovel. "Nah. I figured living next to you, I better dig a bomb shelter. Didn't make it to seventy-nine years old without thinking ahead."

Mom gritted her teeth until they squeaked. "Good luck with that."

He grunted and went back to hammering the ground.

"Silly old coot," Mom muttered. "And don't even think of telling anyone I said that."

"I won't," I promised over the box filled with paper fairies in my arms. I might have crossed my fingers if I could have moved them under my load.

Mr. Parker probably had the right idea, even if he'd left it until too late. I would have dug a shelter myself if I hadn't wasted so much time chasing a father who didn't exist. Now the satellite was almost here, and all I could do was wait for it and keep my mother close.

"If I survive the satellite, I don't s'pose there's any chance of me getting that iguana we talked about?" I asked, passing another fairy to Mom.

I didn't hear her answer, because things suddenly got very loud.

A bone-rattling *boom* crashed through the sky high above our heads.

Panicked birds flapped into the air, where there was a screech.

We both looked upward.

A tiny sun sped through the sky toward us, faster than anything I had ever seen.

Mom jumped from the stepladder and threw herself on top of me.

CHAPTER 25

The very good thing about having a mother who was basically 90 percent fairy was that she didn't weigh much. She covered my body with hers while hollering something I couldn't hear over the whistle-shriek in the sky.

Boom! The ground shuddered. A car alarm went off. Someone screamed—Mrs. Cuthbert? Choking dirt filled the air.

Then nothing moved. I held my breath, trying to feel Mom's heartbeat or her breathing. Anything to tell me she had survived.

"Momma?" I moaned.

Way too slowly, Mom eased herself off me. "Are you okay, Bob?"

I whispered, "I'm not dead, am I?"

Mom looked us both up and down, checking for broken bones and missing parts. "No, you're fine. I think that was the satellite." She wrapped her arms around me and kissed the top of my head—poofy ponytail and all. "NASA couldn't predict their way out of a wet paper bag."

Through the dust came the sounds of slamming doors and running feet as our neighbors poured out into the street. Someone shouted, "It's Shirley and Mary's place. Look!"

All I could see from the porch was a gritty haze.

I looked up.

A cloud of dust and debris rose into the sky, hovering over our house like an angry monster. Grandma burst through the front door and grabbed us both in her arms. "You're okay. Oh, you're both okay!" We let her hug us just as tight as she wanted.

Officer Bugden's siren blared in the distance.

"It actually hit our house," Mom said. "You were right, Bob."

A crowd gathered at our gate, and they all stared at us through the powdered earth that billowed up around us. Mrs. Cuthbert screamed and pointed to Mr. Parker's front lawn. Something rose out of the dirt, shaking off clods of what used to be our yard.

"An alien!"

"The satellite had a passenger!"

Mom grabbed me tight, but only for a second. Even through the messy air, we could see it was only Mr. Parker. He must have tried to lie down in the shallow scrapes he'd made in his front lawn and had gotten covered with flying bits of debris.

"What you all starin' at? Ain't you never seen a man exit his temporary bomb shelter?"

When someone in the crowd let out a chuckle, he cussed at them.

Mom, Grandma, and I looked up at our roof. There it was, glowing a dull red from the smothered sunlight, but in one piece.

"Wait, so it didn't hit us after all?" Mom asked, coughing a bit and shaking her hair out.

"Oh no, it hit you, all right," Mr. Humphries said, pointing at our still neatly trimmed front lawn. There, surrounded by sprays of dried grass and stones, was a hole big enough to make a much better bomb shelter than Mr. Parker's temporary one. It had missed the bull's-eye by at least ten feet but had taken out one of Grandma's poor rosebushes.

"Holy moly." I ran over and flopped onto my belly to peer down into the hole. It was wide enough across that I could have climbed inside. Mom hollered something about being careful, but it was a bit late.

"I see it," I called. Half buried at the bottom of the hole was something hard and metal, about the size of a shoe box—probably the top part of the satellite. The rest would be buried underneath.

Mrs. Cuthbert gave me a pair of oven mitts to wear for protection, and Mr. Humphries held my ankles while I reached in and grabbed the metal. It came free in my hands. Not only that, but there wasn't anything else buried underneath. They hoisted me to my feet, and I held up my prize.

It was a scorched and twisted metal thing the size of a small toaster.

"That's the satellite?"

"It must have burned up on reentry. NASA couldn't have been worried about a toaster!"

"What a lot of fuss over nothing."

The crowd turned and shuffled away through the orange glow of settling space dust.

A tingly feeling worked its way up from my toes and burst onto my face as a huge smile. The part of me that believed in genetic destiny could hardly believe my luck. We were all alive. Mom, Grandma, me, and our house.

I held up the toaster-sized satellite remains, triumphant, as someone took a picture.

CHAPTER 26

The second time I made an appearance on *What's Current,* I was the lead story. It got picked up nationwide, which was a pretty big deal for someone whose greatest achievement was plucking a tiny bit of mangled metal out of the ground. My photo made the front page of every newspaper in the country. Seeing my full name in print didn't bother me a bit anymore, because it was my dad's name too. Sort of.

It wasn't a bad photo either.

Me, surrounded by a dust cloud, holding a lump of nothing much in my hand, with headlines like NASA APOLOGIZES FOR INCONVENIENCE, and NASA CONFIRMS GRAVITY GIRL NABBED LARGEST PIECE OF XR-26, and my personal favorite, NASA FLIES GIRL AND MOM TO COLLECT COMPENSATION CHECK.

A fifty-thousand-dollar apology to make up for the stress and the hole in our lawn.

Sure, the satellite had landed on our property, but the hole only took a few minutes to fill in. Fifty thousand smackeroos could buy a lot of natural food dye and sugar substitutes, though, and at least one cute, if rather bitey, pet iguana. I called him Hugo—because the name had absolutely nothing to do with space.

We got the only compensation check, even though a tiny bit of satellite broke a window in Mrs. Cuthbert's house, and another smashed Dameon Swenson's new bike, which his parents had bought him for his twelfth birthday. Apparently satellites have a keen sense of justice.

So did Mom. She paid for the window and bought Dameon a new bike, even though she didn't have to. Mrs. Cuthbert would probably still make our lives miserable, but like Grandma always said, "It's better to have the moral high ground and a healthy dose of good karma."

Grandma sure talked big for someone who'd sprayed her neighbor with a hose.

Dameon, though, smiled at me a couple of times after he got his new bike. At first, I thought it was a snarl, because of the bared teeth and all, but he kept doing it. Eventually, I realized he wasn't in pain or anything. It might have even been gratitude.

Mom and I stepped out of Mr. Bones's rickshaw after he drove us home from the library, where we had picked up books on raising iguanas. It took some getting used to, worrying about ordinary things like preventing unpro-voked lizard attacks instead of falling space debris.

Mom gave me the biggest hug when she led me inside the house. "I think satellites are good luck, like falling stars," she said.

"And raccoons living under your store," I said.

"Huh?" Mom asked.

"Never mind."

Upstairs, I looked for something to wear that night to the first toddler-free party we'd held at our house in as long as I could remember. There was nothing like a huge check and being alive to make a family want to celebrate. While I searched my limited wardrobe, I let Hugo play on my bed.

I learned one lesson about pet parenting right away: lizards poop like any other pet, only they don't care if they are standing on your bed when they do it. I carried my pillow to the window to shake it out before taking it to the laundry room, but a loud banging from our backyard distracted me. Was Mrs. Cuthbert revenge-tidying the backyard now?

"You stay here, Hugo," I said, setting him on a towel. "Guard the place, and don't you dare poop on anything." I knew he wouldn't listen—he hadn't even learned his name yet—but it was responsible pet ownership to try.

I sped downstairs and into the backyard. The noise was

coming from my headquarters. When I looked up, I saw a wall where things used to be way too open-air. "Hey! What's going on? Who's up there?"

Some muffled laughter came from inside, but no one answered. I went for the ladder—and stopped to stare. Now it was wooden and attached firmly to the trunk of the old elm. No rope, no fraying.

"What the . . . ?" I asked as my head popped through the floor hole.

Smiling down at me were Nickel and his dad, Officer Bugden. Grandma was crouched in the corner, fitting a window frame into the brand-new wall, with her tool belt around her waist. They had hammers, building supplies, and proud expressions.

"You got back a bit early," said Grandma.

"Who knew Mr. Bones could pedal so fast?" Officer Bugden pulled off his work gloves and tucked them into the back of his jeans. "I'll have to keep an eye on him."

"Mom wanted to get here before the party guests," I said, unable to concentrate on anything but the totally un-see-through wall situation. The thing about monumental surprises was that you could never think of something important enough to say in return.

I glanced up at the list of headquarters rules taped to the wall and saw Nickel had crossed *No Boys* off the list.

"We worked all day today," Nickel said, still grinning.

He held out a hand to help me the rest of the way into my rebuilt HQ.

I gazed around at the best thing anyone had ever done for me. Turned out dads were fine things to have, but friends, grandmothers, and brand-new headquarters were pretty good too.

Nickel's dad squeezed himself onto the ladder through the hole in the floor. If I'd be entertaining him in the future, that hole would need widening.

"Thank you," I said, even though they were far too tiny words for something that big.

Grandma passed the tools to Nickel's dad and climbed down after him. "You two better come inside soon. You don't want to miss the party."

I certainly didn't, even if the theme was guaranteed to be smothered in fairy dust. We didn't go right away, though. With satellite cleanup, father revelations, massive checks, and iguanas, we hadn't had a lot of time to catch up.

"So Benjamin O'Malley isn't even a distant relative. How about that?" Nickel said, fidgeting with a bent nail like he'd forgotten how to talk to me. "Sorry about your real dad, though."

I shrugged. "Me too. At least I know."

"And you're not related to Michael. So, yay."

We both giggled at that. Once we laughed, things got

almost normal again, but not quite, because Nickel gave me a hug. It wasn't a kiss, but it was his idea, at least. Finally, he was catching on.

Laughing to myself, I swung my legs down to the ladder.

In front of the house, the grill and tables were set up over the spot where the bull's-eye used to be before the grass started to grow. Nickel's dad and Grandma were jostling for grilling rights, while a few people stood around nibbling fairy cakes and dainty sandwiches. Mr. Bones was flopped in a fold-out chair, swigging on a large iced tea. Mrs. Cuthbert and Mr. Parker sat right by the grill, arguing about the steaks. Mrs. Gilbert, the Humphries family, and a couple of other neighbors sat around too. They had probably just come so they could see if we all glowed in the dark now.

Come to think of it, I needed to check that out myself.

I looked around for Mom, but she was nowhere to be seen. Her touch was everywhere, though. Paper fairies hung around the porch. Glitter twinkled on the tablecloths—but that was probably left over from the hundreds of sparkle-party tables they'd covered.

When Mom did finally come out, more than a dozen bright balloons bobbed along behind her as she skipped down the steps. She handed a red balloon to me. Tied to the string was one of her paper fairies.

Mom gave everyone a balloon to hold and cleared her throat. "Robyn never had a chance to meet her dad, and

he never had a chance to meet her either. So tonight we can help her say goodbye properly. If you could all write down a memory of Byron, if you have one, on your paper fairy, and we'll each read ours out."

Mrs. Humphries went first, after scribbling a note on her fairy. "When he first defected from Densdale and came to live here, Byron stopped to help me change a flat tire. Lovely boy. Fan of beef jerky too."

We all clapped, and the next person stood up.

Everyone took a turn. Even Mrs. Cuthbert. "He knew how to prune a rosebush, I'll give him that," she said.

There were good stories—sad ones too. And funny ones. But Grandma's was my favorite.

"He made my daughter happier than she's ever been, before or since, and gave us our little Miss Sparkles." She kissed her paper fairy and made a little sniffling sound.

I wondered what Mom had been like when he was still here. Another parent I'd never know.

Mom didn't speak. She just shook her head, kissed the note on her fairy, and pressed it to her heart. Somehow, she managed not to cry, which just made it worse. Listening to all the stories of my dad, I felt like I knew him a little bit more. I knew me a bit more too. It was a sort of relief.

Mom handed me a pen and opened the folded fairy on my balloon. "Write what's important to you, Bob."

There wasn't much room, but I didn't have much to say.

I wrote: *We'd have liked each other. Robyn (your daughter, btw) xoxo*

Not much, really, after almost twelve years of not speaking. When I held the balloon out in front of me, I thought of a million excellent things I could have written. I'd have looked silly if I'd scribbled it out and written something else, though. Besides, it would do. My dad would know what I wanted to say.

"You don't have to read it out," Mom said. Then she whispered in my ear, "Red was his favorite color."

I smiled and let the string slip through my fingers until the balloon tugged free and rose into the sky. After a few moments, the others let theirs go too. The balloons all floated straight up after mine, not bobbing anywhere near the house, or the roof, or even me.

" 'How now, spirit? Whither wander you?' " I whispered. "I love you, Dad." I blew the balloons a kiss goodbye, hoping they wouldn't strangle any wildlife. We watched quietly as they disappeared into the cloudless sky.

Then, out of nowhere, a scream.

Way up in the air, someone shrieked the sort of panicked squeal a person made before having their parachute catch on a cast-iron rooster weather vane.

"Oh no!" I grabbed Nickel's hand.

We all ducked or ran for cover.

A screaming woman rode an out-of-control hang glider right past our house. Instead of colliding with the roof,

she looped up and then back down to land on Mrs. Cuthbert's porch roof.

Grandma cracked up. I mean, she cackled like a feuding neighbor with absolutely no moral high ground to stand on. Mrs. Cuthbert picked herself up from where she'd dived under the table and stared slack-jawed at the person struggling to her feet on her roof.

Now I knew what life looked like to a person with a better-than-average chance of not being squashed—because this had to mean that the curse was broken. Forever. Or at least it had moved next door.

"Uh, sorry, folks," the stranded woman called out. "Little help?"

"Looks like you better give that roof of yours a stern talking-to, Abigail," Officer Bugden said, and he winked at me as he hurried off to help.

ACKNOWLEDGMENTS

In 1979, we waited anxiously for a space station called Skylab to crash back to Earth. As a ten-year-old child in possession of quite an imagination, I was utterly convinced I had a personal bull's-eye hovering above my head. I was wrong, obviously, but the whole event left a major impression that helped inspire this book. So thank you, NASA, for terrifying the living daylights out of a mostly innocent child and inspiring her future debut novel.

While the following people may not have made me fear for my life, they've all improved it and helped with this book in many ways: Natalie, who reads all my work and perfected the "Positivity Sandwich." Sara Megibow, who loved this book even when I lost faith. Caroline Abbey, for her wisdom and ability to weed out all my repetitions. Tabitha, who giggled in all the right places. Kathryn, for her efforts to improve my grammar. Kent, for being my beautiful assistant. Dinko, for giving me a most excellent keyboard. Melissa Elliott, for making sure I represented a child with albinism as well as I could. Lisa, for writing a funny book to inspire me. And my big sister, Sheryl, and our nephew Mathew, I wish you were both here to see this.

Lastly, to my kids, Jonny and Emily, who make me so proud that they make me want to be a better person just to compete. To Laura, for hugging my boy when I can't. To Victor, for never remembering which of my books is which, but trying hard. And to Jayden, Grayson, Hunter, and Baxter—my inspirations, my heart, and my biggest distractions. Thank you all.